ABSENT

BY KATIE WILLIAMS

CHRONICLE BOOKS
SAN FRANCISCO

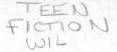

TEEN
FICTION
WIL

FOR ULY

Library of Congress Cataloging-in-Publication Data

Williams, Katie, 1978–
    Absent / by Katie Williams.
        p. cm.
    Summary: Seventeen-year-old Paige Wheeler died in a fall off the high school roof and now her spirit seems bound to the school grounds, along with Brooke and Evan, two other teen ghosts who died there—but maybe if she can solve the mystery of her apparent suicide they will all be able to move on.
    ISBN 978-0-8118-7150-1 (alk. paper)
    1. Ghost stories. 2. Teenagers—Suicidal behavior—Juvenile fiction. 3. Teenagers—Drug use—Juvenile fiction. 4. Suicide—Juvenile fiction. 5. High school students—Juvenile fiction. [1. Ghosts—Fiction. 2. Suicide—Fiction. 3. Drug abuse—Fiction. 4. High schools—Fiction. 5. Schools—Fiction.] I. Title.
    PZ7.W6665811438Abs 2013
    813.6—dc23

                                2012033600

Design by Jennifer Tolo Pierce.
Typeset in Adobe Caslon and Amarelinha.

Manufactured in China.

10 9 8 7 6 5 4 3 2 1

Chronicle Books LLC
680 Second Street, San Francisco, California 94107

www.chroniclebooks.com/teen

PROLOGUE

"WHEN YOU DIE," LUCAS HAYES ONCE TOLD ME, "IT'S LIKE every wound your body has ever had— every skinned knee, paper cut, pimple—opens up and says *See? I told you so.*" Lucas had held Brooke Lee as she'd jittered and bucked, rolled and foamed, and— yeah—died, so I figured he knew what he was talking about.

My best friend, Usha Das, took a different view. "Dying isn't pain," she said. "It's nothing. That's scary now, but you won't feel scared when you're nothing. You'll feel nothing when you're nothing."

The biblicals in their cafeteria prayer circle all agreed that dying was being folded in the arms of Our Father, all woolly beard, thick bathrobe, and water vapor. The burners, on the other hand, hated their fathers, who bothered them all the time. Or didn't bother them enough. They sucked on their cigarettes and said that dying was like blowing out smoke. Then they'd watch their smoke rise and twist and disappear over the heads of the shampoo-shiny ponies and gym-wet testos, who didn't need to think about death because they could just smile pretty at the grim reaper and watch him float the other way, couldn't they?

People were talking a lot about death that year, my senior year, because Brooke Lee had died right there in the girls' bathroom across from the gym. I didn't pay attention to most of it. My classmates were no more than what Usha and I had named them— biblicals, well-rounders, testos, and the rest—and they were always babbling on about one thing or another. But after I died, they started talking about *my* death and then I had no choice but to listen.

1: MARCH GRIEF GROUP MEETING

AT THE MARCH GRIEF GROUP MEETING, MY FORMER CLASSMATES steer their chairs in lazy circles, bumping the armrests against one side of the table, then the other. Posters stare down at them, pouting teen models labeled with pretend afflictions: *Anorexia! Gonorrhea! Steroids! Depression!* On the table, a row of Kleenex boxes issues its scratchy white blossoms. How many tears would it take to soak this supply? How many nose blows? How many muffled sobs? They should advertise on the side of the box: *Good for the average break-up, fourteen sad movies, or the death of a small dog.* Not that anyone here is crying over the death of a small dog. Or the death of a teenage girl. Though I suppose the dog has a better chance of earning a few tears.

We dead kids sit on the floor in the corner of the room: one, two, three. On my left, Evan holds his skinny body upright, like it's a posture contest. On my right, Brooke slumps so far forward that she manages to display the fraying lace of both bra in the front and underwear in the back. I sit between them, knees pulled to chin, the buckles of my boots clinking around my ankles when I shift, like

Marley's chains. The three of us never would have sat together when we were alive.

At least I fold up easily in my soft-skin clothes—old jeans and a velvety jacket from one of Usha's vintage scrounges. She's convinced me to like about used clothes what most people hate: the other bodies that have unstiffened their elbows and knees, stretched out their pockets, salted them with sweat, only to toss the clothes out at the precise moment when they are really ready to be worn. Even the rubber band that holds my hair in a twist at the edge of my vision was scooped off a teacher's desk.

"They'll talk about you now, Paige. You'll see," Brooke whispers.

"Like I care what they say." And I don't. Care. They had one of these grief group meetings after Brooke's death back in September. Now they've added my death to the agenda. Two birds, one stone. Two dead girls, one conference room. I'm only here because Evan kept pestering me to come.

"If you're lucky, maybe they'll say you were friendly and free-spirited." Brooke puts sarcastic emphasis on the words the group has just used to describe her.

"Those were nice things to say," Evan tells her.

"They were nice ways of saying slut," Brooke replies.

Friendly and *free-spirited*—those aren't words my former class-mates will use to describe me. My words probably live in the *S* section of the alphabet: *sarcastic, smart-mouthed, slouchy*.

Usha stares at the fake wood of the conference table. She's wear-ing her mechanic's jumpsuit, the one with the *Orville* nametag on it. I was the one who'd pulled that jumpsuit from the two-dollar bin at the Salvation Army, but I let her have it because she'd held it up to herself and twirled. I wasn't the twirling type of girl, but Usha was. Or at least she used to be. Since my death, she's been the tabletop-staring type of girl. I wish I could tell her that I'm okay. I wish I could tell her that I miss her.

I catalog the other faces around the table. Next to Usha perches the gaggingly beautiful Kelsey Pope, who tears out a strip of notebook paper and begins to fold it into an origami flower. By the end of the meeting, that flower is going to be tucked behind her petal of an ear; you can bet on it. I'm surprised to see Kelsey here because it's not like we were friends. Maybe she wants people to think she is deep. Maybe she wrote a poem about it. At the foot of the table, shaggy-haired Wes Nolan fingers something in his pocket, obviously something forbidden—a lighter, a little bag of pot, a folding knife. Everyone knows he's only here to get out of class.

All in all, fifteen of my former classmates have gathered for one final chance to memorialize Brooke and me. Fifteen out of the 632 students at Paul Revere High School. What percentage is that? I start to do the math in my head, but stop because I already know the number will be pathetically low.

And then there are the people who didn't bother to come at all.

Lucas Hayes, for example.

Not that I expected him to.

"Paige Wheeler." Mrs. Morello, the guidance counselor, stretches my name until it's completely out of shape. She wears a blue sweater as if we were little kids for whom red means anger, pink means love, and blue means sadness. "Who would like to share a memory about Paige?"

Nothing.

Not a word.

Not that I care.

I close my eyes, and the silence becomes a noise rushing under everything, like a TV set to static in the other room. If I listen carefully, I can almost hear another sound, one *beneath* the silence. My name. It's as if a dozen people are whispering it in a string: *Paige, Paige, Paige, Paige.*

"Right here," I almost say. "I'm right here."

Mrs. Morello clears her throat, but this prompts no one to speak. We're closing in on a minute now. People always call for a minute of silence, but really a minute is a long time when you're—scuffling, whispering, fidgeting—alive. And a minute is forever when you're shaking on the bathroom floor or standing on the lip of a roof, the miniature world arranged so carefully below you. You feel like you could live in that minute forever, like it would stretch its bounds for you, its sixty tick-ticks, and hold your entire life.

But a minute always ends.

"I didn't know her much."

I look around to see who has finally spoken before realizing that the voice is coming from the end of the table. Wes Nolan.

Everyone glares at Wes like he's just farted or belched or whooped with joy, and I know they're thinking—because I'm thinking it, too—*What are you even doing here, Wes Nolan?* Wes leans back in his chair, grinning his cantilevered grin like he enjoys making a target of himself.

"But I wish I'd known her better," he adds.

I look to Usha, hoping that she'll say something about me. Usha knows me better than anyone. We've been best friends since seventh grade, when the cafeteria tables somehow squared up without us. After a week sitting alone at a table meant for twenty, I noticed this chubby Indian girl brown-bagging it in front of her locker. We weren't supposed to have food outside of the cafeteria, but when the hall monitor paused to tell the girl so, she looked at him with such a determined grin—the kind of grin kids pull for the camera, more teeth than smile—that he unpaused without saying a word. Then she swung her grin to me; I might have walked the other way, too, except just then she reached into her sack and came up with an apple slice. Maybe that's the memory Usha will share, how in seventh grade we crunched apple slices, and how every day for five years after that, the two of us ate lunch cross-legged on the floor in front of our lockers.

But no. Usha doesn't say anything. She just stares at her tabletop.

Kelsey Pope speaks up instead, her hazel eyes shiny as tumbled stones, her cheek piercing winking in the UV light. "I can't help but think we could have been friends, Paige and I." She tucks the origami flower behind her ear.

I make a noise too sharp to be a laugh. Evan and Brooke look over. "Friends with Kelsey Pope?" I say. "Not hardly. Not ever."

"It's just so tragic," Kelsey continues, and the others nod sagely at this wisdom. "I can't imagine ever feeling sad enough to . . . oh. Nothing. Never mind." Kelsey bites on her lip, a pouty pink stopper for her sentence.

Suddenly, the silence becomes *still*. People stop spinning the chairs. Their eyes connect and disconnect across the table. "I told you," a girl I don't know whispers to her friend. I turn to the dead kids. Evan's expression has gone flatter than usual. Brooke rakes her fingers through her ponytail.

"Sad enough to what?" I ask, just as Wes says, "Never mind what?"

Kelsey unstoppers her mouth. "I shouldn't say anything." She sucks in her lips, pooches them out again. "Up on the roof, she . . ."

Kelsey trails off. Usha has finally raised her eyes from the table top and fixed them on Kelsey with a ferocious glare. Before Kelsey can say another word, Usha pushes her chair away from the table with a screech and marches out of the room. We all look after her.

"Oh, no," someone breathes.

"Sad enough to what?" I repeat, my voice too loud in my own ears. "Up on the roof, I what?"

"I think maybe she's saying—" Evan begins, but Mrs. Morello talks over him. "Everyone. Please. The official cause of death was *an accidental fall.*" She says it like she's reading off a script.

"Of course it was an accident," I say. "What else would it have been?"

The bell rings a wordless answer to my question, and everyone rises, hoisting backpacks, fishing for cell phones, and wandering out. Mrs. Morello hurries after them, waving a half-signed attendance sheet. In a matter of seconds, the room is empty.

Empty but for us dead kids.

Evan, Brooke, and I look at each other across the detritus of the meeting—shredded tissues, the origami flower, a forgotten pen.

"Sad enough to jump," I say. "That's it, isn't it? She was saying I killed myself."

I wait for them to deny it. They don't. Evan reaches out to touch my arm, never mind that we can't touch each other. But I don't want comfort, his or anyone's. I take a step back.

"I wouldn't do that," I say. "Even if I were sad enough to think of it, I wouldn't be so . . ."

"So what?" Evan asks.

"So weak."

Evan drops his hand to his side. My eyes follow its trajectory, and I picture a girl standing on the edge of a roof. I picture her stepping off, one foot and then the next, and then an empty space where she had been. I squeeze my eyes shut and shake my head. I feel like I'm falling now, the sick swoop of gravity in my throat and gut. My eyes land on Usha's empty chair, thrust out farther than the others.

"Usha thinks I jumped," I say. "Did you see her face?"

"Paige," Evan murmurs.

"It doesn't matter what Morello tells them about accidents. They'll all keep saying it. It'll go around the whole school. Everyone will hear it." *Lucas will hear it*, a mean little corner of my mind whispers. "Oh, God. Do you think it'll get back to my parents?"

"No," Evan says immediately. "No way. It's just kids gossiping."

"But what if it does? It could. As long as they think . . . they all think . . . ," I sputter out.

"I thought you didn't care what they think," Brooke says quietly.

I pick Brooke's words up and pull them to myself like flat sheets of armor. "You're right. I don't care at all."

2: THE BURNERS' CIRCLE

"I'M NOT EVEN THE SUICIDE TYPE," I SAY.

"The suicide type?" Evan raises an eyebrow.

"You know. Black-haired girls with blond roots and notebooks full of poems with the word *crepuscular* in them. Or guys who wear all beige and won't talk unless it's about their Japanese sword collection, and then they won't stop talking."

"I don't know," Brooke says. "You kinda look like the type to me." She stares pointedly at my feet.

"What? They're just boots! I like all the buckles."

"I think maybe there isn't a suicide type," Evan says.

We've gathered to the side of the hallway, clear of the students rushing from this class to that. Brooke stands at the drinking fountain, her hand pressed to the spigot. A testo from the wrestling team lumbers up and pushes the button, making the water arc straight through Brooke's palm, unimpeded, into the steel drain. This is not to say that Brooke is translucent. In fact—tight-jeaned, liquid-eyelined, licorice-whip of a ponytail—she appears solid as anything. But the water pierces her hand all the same. The testo bends to drink, taking only a sip before he backs away with a grimace.

Brooke cackles. "Look! My hand makes the water taste funny."

Evan shakes his head. "Don't start trouble."

But all Brooke wants to do is start trouble, just as much as Evan wants to prevent it, just as much as I don't care what either of them does.

"He's the third one in a row who wouldn't drink." Brooke turns to the bustling hallway and cries like a barker, "Water here! Get your fresh water!"

"It's just a rumor," Evan tells me. "They'll get tired of it once someone starts a new rumor."

"But even if they stop gossiping about it, they'll still think it," I say. "That's how I'll be remembered: Paige the Jumper. Paige the Suicide Case."

"Look on the bright side," Brooke says. "Eventually they'll all graduate."

"I was going to graduate, go to college." I sigh. "Maybe no one told the schools that I died. Maybe they'll still send the letters. Maybe they're holding a spot for me somewhere."

"Where did you apply?" Evan asks.

"Oregon State, Washington State, USC."

Brooke has stopped with her drinking fountain and is staring at me strangely. When I meet her gaze, her eyes flit away. Maybe I shouldn't talk about colleges in front of Brooke. Even if she hadn't died, she probably wouldn't have applied anywhere. According to the gossip, her interests were in activities other than the academic. What happens to a girl like Brooke after high school?

"They're all on the other side of the country," Evan notes.

"I wanted to go somewhere else. Leave Michigan. Leave here. And now," I gesture at our surroundings, "here I am."

"Here we are," Brooke echoes.

"It's not so bad." Evan turns and looks at the hall, the flow and burble of students rushing by us. "I mean, it could be worse. We have classes and the library and people all around us."

I open my mouth to say something sarcastic about the meager joys of still having *high school*, but then Evan adds, "We have each other." And I decide to shut up because until Brooke arrived in September, Evan was here alone. For how long, he won't say.

"You get used to it," Evan says, like he can read my mind. "You're already getting used to it."

Brooke raises an eyebrow. "Settle in for the world's longest detention."

It's the same thing I'd told myself: that I was getting used to it, coming to terms, or whatever nonsense phrase Mrs. Morello might use for it. But suddenly I feel . . . what? Unsettled. Unfinished. Restless. A restless ghost. Why? Because of some stupid rumor? The phrase "accidental fall" spoken in Mrs. Morello's emphatic tone repeats in my head. I feel it all over again, the giddy dread of my foot stepping back and finding no ground under it.

The bell rings, interrupting my thoughts.

"Come to Fisk's class with me," Evan urges.

"No thanks."

"Then I'll go with you."

I raise my eyebrows. "You? Skip class?" Evan considers it his sworn duty to attend each and every class period, even though his name doesn't appear on any roster. Brooke, on the other hand, brags that she hasn't attended a full class since she was alive. The best part of being dead, she claims.

Evan shrugs, his shoulders rising and falling in precise intervals. "They're playing dodgeball in the gym. Maybe we can see someone lose a tooth again."

"You looked like you were gonna puke last time that happened."

"Well, this time I'll close my eyes and think of the tooth fairy."

"Go to class, Evan," I say. "I'm immune to your attempts at cheer-upped-ness."

Evan looks skeptical. "You sure?"

"Allergic, in fact." I take a step backward. "If it makes you happy, I'll go to class, too."

"Why anyone would willingly go to class," Brooke mutters.

"I think they're dissecting frogs today in junior bio," I say.

"And *that* cheers you up?" Evan asks.

"I find it therapeutic." The school is lousy with ghost frogs, chloroformed for dissection. Beige, green, leopard-spotted, they gather in the corners of the basement, croaking softly, blinking their marbled eyes, and hopping through the cinder-block walls.

"If you're sure," Evan says, clearly relieved to have gotten out of dodgeball.

"Sure I'm sure. Maybe we can find the new frogs tonight. We can say to them, 'You must have been so sad, frog.'" I imitate Kelsey's tremulous voice. "'What friends we might have been.'"

I've lied to Evan. I have no intention of attending a class where I've already been marked permanently, irrevocably, absent. As soon as he turns the corner, I head out to the student parking lot, telling myself I'm just looking for some fresh air (air that I can't even breathe), telling myself I'm just looking for the sun (sun hidden behind spring storm clouds), telling myself I'm not (definitely not) looking for Lucas Hayes.

On my way to the burners' circle, I balance atop the cement stoppers that line the lot. Just after my death—three weeks ago now—I couldn't have balanced like this, couldn't even have walked down the school hall without sinking through the tiles, down to the basement where finally the earth would've stopped my fall with its sediments, its fossils, its underground rivers, and—deep below— its glowing, churning core.

I spent the first week after my death stuck on the packed-dirt floor of the school basement, surrounded by an army of croaking ghost frogs. I sat in their midst, sometimes crying, sometimes rocking, sometimes staring vacantly at the skinny freckled boy who would sit across from me speaking, in patient tones, words that I couldn't stand to hear. Then one day, for no good reason, I felt like I could bear to see the world again. But when I tried to mount the first step of the stairs, my foot sank straight through it, back down to the dirt, where I suppose I now belong.

It took Evan nearly forever to teach me how to suspend myself just millimeters above the school floor (or a set of stairs or the seat of a chair) so that I could approximate the postures of life. *Hovering*, he calls it. Even now, if I don't use a tiny corner of my mind to hold myself just so, I will sink until I hit the earth, however far below that might be. Now, only weeks later, I can hover pretty easily. It was easy once I figured out it wasn't so different from the ways in which life requires you to hold yourself just so.

I've become so adept at hovering that I can, with concentration, jump from one cement stopper to the next, which I do all the way to the adjacent soccer field. I tread out across the field, as close to the burners' circle as I can get. The circle is just a cluster of trees earning their leaves back in patches, a spotty effect like a Boy Scout sash only half-filled with badges.

Lucas Hayes was in Boy Scouts when he was little. He told me when we met among those trees on the day before I died. He could still list off all the badges he'd earned, he said. "Prove it," I said, and so he had, from American Heritage to Wilderness Survival. As he spoke, he assembled my physics project, twisting the strands of wire into the cardboard box. He gave one of the wires a new twist with the name of each badge.

"You're *still* a Boy Scout." I nudged him with my shoulder, the tree bark rasping against the back of my jacket. The snow was still on the ground, except in the burners' circle, where the tree branches held it off of us, as if this place were set aside for us, preserved.

"Careful." He lifted the box. "There's an egg in here, you know."

"Yes, I know. It's *my* project you hijacked. Besides, you're doing it all wrong." He hadn't been, but I could twist the wires just as well as he could.

He handed the project back to me with his flashbulb smile.

"See? Like this," I said.

"For the record, I'm not a Scout anymore. I dropped out in sixth grade."

"Well, maybe you're not a Scout, but you're still Scout-like. Admit it, you still have that sash."

"It was a vest, actually, and really, I'm not as good as all that."

"Why? Because you have a secret—" I bit down on my sentence.

I'd almost said *girlfriend*, which I was not. Not at all. We'd agreed on that from the start. Who needed the looks in the hallway? Not to mention the gossip. Besides, it was no big deal. He was just a stupid testo.

A stupid testo who happened to be good at kissing.

Fortunately, Lucas didn't seem to have heard my slip. "Come on," I babbled for cover. "You're captain of the whatever team."

"You know it's basketball," he said. "And baseball in the spring."

"You get good grades," I continued, "probably mostly by smiling at the teachers. Yeah, that's the smile I mean. And on top of it all, you're the school hero. You practically saved a girl's life."

Lucas's smile shut off. "Don't say that."

"Why not?"

"Because I *didn't* save her."

And it was true. Lucas had called for help when he found her, but by the time they'd gotten there, Brooke Lee was dead. An overdose. Cocaine.

"Sorry," I murmured. And I was.

"How about you?" Lucas said, his smile back, though at half wattage. "Were you a Girl Scout?"

"Nope. Not me. I'm not much for dressing identically and earning badges."

"That reminds me. I forgot to mention one other thing I earned a badge for." He leaned close, the cloud of his breath puffing against my face. I should have earned a badge for not wincing at Lucas's pick-up lines.

"A kissing badge, huh? How'd you practice your skill? On the troop leader or the other little boys?" I inquired of his puckered-up face.

"You're sick, Paige Wheeler."

"The sickest," I said happily.

"I like that about you."

"Yeah, right."

"I do." He paused, looking suddenly serious. "You don't mind, do you?"

"Mind that you messed up my physics project?"

"Mind being my secret."

So he *had* heard me almost say "secret girlfriend." I could feel the blood lighting up my cheeks, and I silently cursed my pallor. Kelsey Pope, Lucas's ex-girlfriend, tanned herself to a crisp year round; no one ever knew when she was embarrassed. If she ever had anything to be embarrassed about, that is.

"I don't mind," I told Lucas. "After all, you're my secret, too."

He smiled at this and touched my blood-lit cheek.

This time, I let him kiss me.

And I didn't even think about wincing.

The opposite, in fact.

When we pulled away, Lucas got up and walked to the edge of the trees, scanning the soccer field and parking lot for people. He glanced back at me before stepping out.

"I'll go first," he said. "You'll wait a few minutes?" He left the rest unspoken: *So no one will see us together.*

I stayed among the trees and watched him walk across the field, his footsteps pressing through the snow. When I walked out after him, I'd leave my footsteps behind me, too. It struck me that someone later, seeing them, would imagine two people walking side by side.

Today, the trees of the burners' circle stand tall and silent. I can't go in, but I can see that no one is sneaking out from between their trunks. Behind me, a door bangs open, and I turn. Three freshman boys clump by the far doors of the school. With a shove, they send one of their number into the parking lot. He ventures to a patch of tar that's darker than the rest of the blacktop. When he reaches it, he bends down and touches it. His friends hoot in approval, and he runs back with a triumphant smile, his hand held in the air like a lit torch.

A dare to touch it.

The school door opens again, startling the boys. When they see who it is, they slide into a tighter group, feigning nonchalance. The boy who touched the patch of tar hides his hand behind his back, even though the tar dried weeks ago and his fingers are unmarked.

Lucas Hayes lopes out, followed by two of his testo teammates, laughing about something one of them said on the other side of the doors. When Lucas didn't show up at today's grief group, I'd secretly hoped that he was sitting out here in our circle of trees. A grief group meeting of one. But the truth is as plain as the laughter on his face. It'll be all over the school by now, the rumor that I jumped. Has Lucas heard it? Does he believe it?

Lucas parts from his friends and continues across the lot on his own. I watch carefully as he passes the burners' circle, and my breath catches when he glances at it. At me. I imagine him saying my name close to my ear. *Paige.* But then his eyes flick over me and onto the road. Of course he can't see me. And really, it's not so different from the times before my death when we would pass in the cafeteria or the hall and his eyes would move past me. No, through me.

I catch up to him at the edge of the lot and stand next to him on the frosty hunch of grass that separates school from road. A steady stream of minivans flows past the school. As Lucas waits for a break in the traffic, I study his profile, remembering how sometimes he'd reach over and pluck an object from the ground—a bent twig, an abandoned lighter, a skeletal leaf—and gaze at it with guileless eyes. He looked at everything in the world like it was a present he'd just opened. And it was heady, being lifted from your wrappings and looked at anew, just as much as it was infuriating, the invisible tag with his name on it.

"I didn't like you," I say, even though he can't hear me. "I just liked kissing you. You know that, right?"

And then something possesses me, and I reach over and grab his hand. As I do, Lucas turns and looks back at the burners' circle. Underneath the rush of afternoon traffic, I hear it again. *Paige.*

And my hand.

It bumps against his.

It catches.

I'm not saying that I'm holding Lucas's hand. I'm not saying that. But instead of passing through, my hand settles in his like it's found a pocket of space where it fits. I stare down at it. When I was alive, Lucas and I never held hands.

I start to feel something in the center of me dissolving like sugar into water, like snow on the pavement, like my body when Lucas kissed me deep. But just as the feeling starts to grow, Lucas turns and spots a break in the traffic. He leaps off the curb, his hand falling free of mine. Before I know it, he's disappeared between the houses across the street.

I step off the curb after him, across the invisible property line that separates school grounds from the rest of the world. But unlike Lucas, my feet don't land on the blacktop of the street in front of me. Instead, with one small step, I find myself hundreds of feet back and three stories above where I just was. I now stand on the lip of the school roof.

3: A LESSON FROM THE SCHOOL SLUT

THE FEELING IN BETWEEN THE CURB AND THE ROOF, EVEN though it lasts only a moment, isn't a pleasant one. It's a flattening, separating, pressing feeling, like a meager pat of butter scraped thin over burnt toast. Once it's over, I feel lumped back together again, but all wrong. I open my eyes and look down at the parking lot below. I scuff my shoes against the cement lip that runs foot-high around the edge of the school roof. A safety feature. Ha.

I don't have to think about holding myself in place here on the roof's ledge. I don't have to worry about hovering. Besides the soil of the earth, this is the only spot in the school where the world can touch me and I can touch it. I didn't die from hitting the ground; I died from hitting my head right here on this ledge. This little section of concrete is where my skull cracked and the shards of bone pushed themselves up into the squish of my brain, stopping its flashes and flickers. My death spot.

I let the soles of my boots relax onto the cement, let the breeze pick up the stray bits of hair that have eternally escaped my rubber band. A curl of ivy grows from a crack in the cement at my feet; on its end, a tiny pointed green leaf. I reach down and pluck it, just because I can. Though as soon as I pull it from its vine, the little leaf drifts through the tips of my fingers and down to the parking lot below. I wish I'd let it alone to keep growing.

Each time I step over the school's property line, I end up back here. Just like when Brooke steps over the school property line, she appears on the floor of the school bathroom or Evan on the seal of the gym floor. When we try to escape, the school takes us back to where we died. Our death spots.

I look out at the neighborhood across the road. My house is over there, too far away to see, small and green with dark red trim, colors my father always threatened to paint over. When I was little, I begged him not to. *The Christmas House*, that's what the kids at school called it, and it had felt special to live in a house with such a name. As I'd grown older, the specialness had worn off, the colors reverting themselves to simple green and red. At some point, I'd stopped protesting when my father talked about how any day now he'd repaint the house. *Just do it*, I'd finally said. *You keep talking about it.* After that, he'd never mentioned it again. It occurs to me now that maybe the real reason my father had kept saying he'd repaint the house was just to hear me ask him not to.

There are so many things to lose.

I search the horizon for the house that I can't even see. I think again of my parents. Will someone tell them what Kelsey said at the grief group meeting? Will they think that I killed myself? Even if they don't believe it, would a tiny part of them wonder if it was true? I imagine their faces the saddest I've ever seen them, my father's brow folded up into wrinkles, the sound of my mother's crying, small expulsions of breath like she's being punched in the stomach again and again.

The thought takes my feet out from under me. I sit down and drop my head into my hands, wishing my death spot would allow for tears. I come here when it rains anyway, turn my face up and let the drops plink on my cheeks. The moment I step off my death spot and back onto the roof, I'm dry again, like the rain never was. I lift my face from my hands, scanning the clouds for dark spots, for flickers of lightning.

"Thought you'd be up here," a voice says behind me.

I turn. Brooke sits on the cage of one of the whirring industrial fans, inspecting a hole in her jeans.

"I hate these jeans, you know? But that morning, everything else was unwearably dirty. Leave it to me to OD on laundry day." She works her finger around the frayed edge of the hole. "I had this other pair I wish I could be wearing. People wrote all over them. Everyone I know wrote on them. Like I was famous."

I remember those jeans, the denim faded to a soft parchment. And she isn't exaggerating. Nearly every inch of them was covered in messages, signatures, and doodles. And when I say every inch, I mean even the butt, even the inner thighs. People said it was the guys she had sex with who got signature space there. It was the school joke: sign the slut. She must not know about that part.

"I wonder where they are now," she says. "My mom probably burned them. She was always threatening to."

"You don't think she would keep them?" I picture my own mom standing in front of my closet jammed with musty thrift-store finds. She wouldn't throw anything away. She'd keep it all on the hangers.

"When I was alive, I wanted everything to change. Now it never will. Same stupid hole in my jeans. Same stupid school."

Brooke hops down from the fan and crosses the roof to where I sit on the ledge. She peers over the side. We both look at the ground below.

"I've done it, you know," she says. "I've jumped."

"Off a *roof?*"

"Off this roof."

I feel cold, like the wind isn't hitting me anymore, but rushing straight through me. "When?"

"After you died. I wondered what it felt like for you."

"Did it hurt when you hit the ground?" I ask.

"Did it hurt for you?" she asks back, her voice cracking on the word *hurt.*

"I wasn't awake for that part. I hit here." I touch the roof's ledge. The cement shows no stain of blood, no chip of bone, no sign I was even there. "That hurt. But it also . . . the whole thing felt like I was watching it happen. Like I was watching myself slip. Fall. They say that's what shock feels like."

I look up from the ground and out across the parking lot, the last bits of winter's snow piled and rock-riddled like scraps left on a plate.

"Did it hurt when you OD'd?" I ask.

"Yeah."

"Did it feel like you were watching it happen?"

"It felt like I was watching stupid Lucas Hayes lean over me, trying to get his cell phone out of his bag. Then he stared at it forever, and I was, like, *Dial 911. How hard is that?* Not that I could manage to tell him that, since I was busy going into cardiac arrest at the time. What's his excuse?"

"He was probably scared," I say.

"Scared of getting in trouble," she says.

"It must have been a shock to walk in on."

"A shock to walk in on," she repeats. "Yeah, that must have been real traumatic for Lucas compared to, you know, *dying*." She studies me. "Did he tell you that? That he was in shock?"

"I didn't really, you know, know him or anything," I say.

"Stop."

"Stop what?"

"Lying. I know about you and Lucas. I used to watch you."

"I don't know what you mean," I mumble.

She ticks off on her fingers. "I mean the notes he put in your locker, the secret looks in the hall, the trips out there." She points to the burners' trees, tiny across the black stretch of parking lot. "Of course I couldn't follow you there." And she couldn't have. It's across the school property line; that's why the burners meet there to smoke. "But I have an imagination and, if you believe the gossip, plenty of experience with that kind of thing."

"We didn't . . . we only . . . we only kissed," I splutter. I shake my head. "You *knew*?" I'm not sure how I feel. Relieved? I think I feel relieved. "No one knew. I didn't even tell Usha."

"Why not? Wasn't she your best friend or something?"

"It was no big deal." I leave the other reasons unspoken: that I didn't know how to explain it, me hooking up with some testo.

The testo. The celebrated Lucas Hayes, Mr. Slam Dunk, Mr. Gleam Tooth. And then, the reason I only sometimes admitted, that if the truth had gotten out, it would have been over. Lucas wouldn't have wanted to meet me anymore.

Brooke eyes me like she knows all my reasons anyhow. "So Lucas never told you about how he stood there and watched me die?"

"Sometimes he said things that . . . I know he wished he could have done something."

"Something," Brooke echoes. "Or nothing."

"He was scared. He tried."

"Just like he tried to be your boyfriend?"

"I never asked him for that. It wasn't a big deal with labels and corsages and things. I'm not that type of girl."

"Did he make you memorize that little speech?" she asks bitterly.

"I'd think if anyone would understand, it'd be you."

"Why? Because I was the school slut? At least I wouldn't pretend not to know someone because it would hurt my reputation."

"He wasn't doing that," I say, but it sounds weak even to me.

For a long moment, we stare out across the street at the houses lit up for the night. Tiny yellow windows. You have no idea how warm those lights are until you're outside the circle of their glow.

"Brooke?"

"Yeah?"

"When you were watching us?"

"Yeah?"

"Did it look like . . . ? Did it seem like Lucas . . . ?" I give up.

"Did it look like he liked you?" Brooke asks for me.

"Not that it matters," I mumble.

Brooke's laugh is dark enough to douse a few of those lights across the street. "Here's a lesson from the school slut: They always look that way when they're kissing you."

I don't know what to say to that. We stand in silence.

"It's not so bad, you know," Brooke finally says, "having them think things about you that aren't true. They all think I was a druggie."

"Brooke. You died of a cocaine overdose."

"I wasn't a druggie, though. I only tried it a couple of times."

"Really? That's it?"

"That's it. It's like a ridiculous after-school special: The chick gets pregnant the first time she has sex, the kid crashes the first time he drives drunk, the girl dies . . ."

She doesn't finish the last one. Her mouth twitches, like only a fraction of the smile can make it through. "I'm just saying, we're dead now. What does it matter what they say? How is it any different from what they said about us when we were alive?"

You're right, I should say. *It doesn't matter about them.* But I can't quite get the words out, so I don't say anything, just pick out patches of dark across the road, trying to guess which house will be the next to turn on its lights.

4: FAIRNESS

WHEN I EMERGE FROM THE STAIRWELL THAT LEADS DOWN from the roof, the extracurriculars are ending, just in time for everyone to get home for dinner. I linger at the ragged edges of groups of student council officers, basketball players, half the chorus for the spring musical, and the track-and-field runners. In one short walk down the school hall, I hear my name mentioned again and again. Everyone is talking about what Kelsey Pope said in the grief group meeting, about how I killed myself.

By the time I reach the end of the hall, I'm sick of my own name. But when I hear it one more time, coming out of the art room's half-open door, I stop, because this time it's Mrs. Morello's voice saying it. I peer in to find her teetering on one of the stools that line the high tables. Mr. Fisk, the art teacher, sits on the stool next to her. Across from them sits Usha.

I can't see Usha's face, only the back of her messy black bob and the tips of her elbows peeking out from either side of her rounded back. Her arms must be crossed over her chest, which is not how

Usha sits at all. Usha sits legs akimbo, head tilted, hands constantly in motion, tapping on the table or her own knees, unless she has pencil and paper, in which case, they're busy drawing. I step closer to this tough-jawed, pulled-up version of Usha.

"... authorized a mural to memorialize the students we've lost this year," Mrs. Morello is saying. "We've designated a section of wall in the hallway. Right by the doors to the student parking lot."

A memorial mural.

I imagine my face floor-to-ceiling high, my painted pupils staring down at students who rush below it. I imagine two girls, decades from now, pausing beneath it. One of them will say, "Who's that?" And her friend will shrug and answer, "Some girl who died." And I'll be standing behind them, silent as my mouth painted on the wall.

Some girl.

Who died.

Mrs. Morello is beaming down at Usha, the kind of lipless smile adults use when they have a present hidden behind their backs. Usually something you don't want. Usually socks.

"The school board decided that, rather than hire a professional artist, it would mean more to have a student paint it. It would be a way to—"

"No," Usha says.

Mrs. Morello blinks rapidly. "Pardon?"

I'm startled, too. Usha isn't a suck-up well-rounder, but she's never rude to teachers. In fact, she was always telling me that it's rude to raise my hand only to point out when a teacher has made a mistake.

"You were going to ask me to do it, right?" Usha asks Mrs. Morello in the same detached voice. "Paint it?"

"Well. Yes."

"So, no. I don't want to paint your mural."

"But . . ." Mrs. Morello's smile falters, then regains its ground. "It's not *my* mural. It's for Paige. Principal Bosworth has decided that you'll have complete creative freedom. Whatever you think best expresses Paige and Brooke and the school's loss, you can paint it. And Mr. Fisk recommended you especially." She looks over at Mr. Fisk for help.

He runs a hand over his beard and clears his throat. "Think of it this way, Usha. This is a chance for you to remember Paige, to help other people remember who she was."

"Maybe we shouldn't be trying so hard to remember her," Usha says. "Maybe we should be trying to forget her."

"Usha," I whisper, even though I know she can't hear me. The world starts to tilt; I look down. I've forgotten my hover and started to sink through the floor. By the time I get my feet right, Mr. Fisk is saying something that ends with ". . . can be upsetting," and Usha has already slid off her stool. She stands with the table between her and the teachers.

"Everyone keeps saying that," she tells him.

"Saying what?" Mr. Fisk asks.

"That word: *upset*. You must be *upset*. Isn't this *upsetting*?"

"Because people are worried about you," Mrs. Morello puts in.

"Well, it's a stupid word. *Upset*. Like something's been knocked off a table. Like *I've* been knocked off a table." She looks down at her crossed arms, takes a breath, uncrosses them, plants them on her hips. "What if I'm not? Upset?"

"Then you're not upset," Mr. Fisk says smoothly. "You can feel whatever you feel."

"I feel angry."

"Yes." Mrs. Morello nods emphatically. "It's not fair, is it?" She pats the table as if Usha's hand were under hers, even though it's not. "It's not fair that she died."

"It's fair." Both adults open their mouths, but Usha keeps talking right over them. "You jump off a roof, you die. That's completely fair."

"Depression can be difficult to—" Morello begins.

"That's the thing," Usha interrupts. "She didn't say she was depressed. She didn't say anything, that she was sad or . . . she just did it. I'm not angry at death. I'm angry at her. I was supposed to be her friend, and she just did it."

"Usha. Please. I didn't." My voice is loud in the quiet room, but it doesn't matter. I could scream, and it wouldn't even be a whisper.

Usha doesn't even flinch as she says to Morello and Fisk, "Sorry, but I'd rather not paint some mural. Not for you, not for the school, and not for her."

5: NO HEAVENLY LIGHT

IN LIFE, USHA WAS MY FRIEND. IN DEATH, EVAN IS. WE SPEND most nights in the library. Though the room is set windowless in the center of the ground floor, it glows with a series of dim lamps that the librarian leaves on; she also leaves books open on the tables and cart. Each night, Evan and I move from one book to the next, reading two pages about photosynthesis, then the French-Indian War, then how to build a go-cart, then a teen romance novel. We shout to each other from across the room: *Found one on economics! Here's, oh,* Little Women, *the haircut scene!* Sometimes I suspect that the librarian leaves the books open on purpose because she knows we're here, but Evan says that's silly. No one knows we're here except for us.

When I arrive in the library that night, I don't tell Evan what Usha said about me. If I say it out loud, I'll . . . I don't know what. Can't cry. Not an option. No working tear ducts. So I pretend it didn't happen. Not just Usha refusing to paint the mural—all of it. I pretend I didn't fall, didn't die. I pretend that my friend Evan and I are staying late to work on a project for school, that we were accidentally locked in the library. We'll pass the time reading random passages out loud until, in the morning, the janitor will open the door to find us blinking in the early light. He'll say, "What are you two doing in here?"

Once Evan and I have finished our snippets of reading, we meet up at the empty spot on the far side of the stacks where the card catalog used to be. The carpet is still tamped down in a square from the old catalog's weight, and we settle into this depression. How much did they weigh, all those slips of paper? Even the ink printed on them must have weighed something.

"Look!" Evan points at the light fixture. A moth flutters around it. "I used to stick the neck of my desk lamp out my window at night just to see the moths do that."

"That's depressing."

"Why?" Evan asks.

"Because. They think they see something beautiful, but they can't get to it. They hit the glass. They keep hitting it until either they knock themselves out or they get fried."

He considers this. "I don't know. I like their optimism."

We both watch the moth for a minute, batting its head and wings against the light fixture.

"Evan? How long have you been here?"

"A long time," he says, which is always his answer. He won't tell me how long he's been here, and he won't tell me how he died. His clothes are the normal sort—jeans, sneakers, a wool sweater—but there's something vaguely outdated about them, like items Usha and I might pass over in the Goodwill bin. Otherwise, he's skinny and freckly, his hair parted in a tidy line. He looks like a teenager, but who knows how old he really is.

"Do you think there's something after this?" I ask.

"I don't know," he says. "No heavenly light has ever shone for me."

"You believe in that, then? In heaven?"

He looks at me sidelong. "Do you?"

"I never went to church." I snort. "Maybe *that's* why I'm stuck here."

"Well, I went to church. Or rather, I was required to go."

"So you believe in God and all that?"

He taps a finger against his bottom lip. "I found church to be an unreliable source. I liked some of what they had to say. Other things, I didn't."

"You mean about gay people?"

His eyes widen, and I immediately wish I could unsay it. I've known since I first met him, something in his movement, his words, his sense of humor, his quality of kindness. Some people you don't know for sure, or you think you do, but then you're wrong. With Evan, it's unmistakable. It's part of who he is.

"I'm not . . ." He shakes his head.

"It's okay," I say. "It's no big deal. Lots of people . . . Usha made out with a girl at summer camp once, and lots of other people are gay . . . or whatever. There's an after-school club, an official one, with an adviser. It's your favorite, actually, Mr. Fisk, and—"

"I'm just not that interested in—" He winces. "I'm more interested in the world of the mind. I don't even have a body, so why should I think about that other stuff? Right?"

"Sure." I think about how much I still think about Lucas and *that other stuff.* How when I think about it now, it's almost like I have a body again.

We're quiet then, quiet enough that I can hear the books around me creaking in their shelves, rustling their pages, stretching their spines, as if they have something to add to the conversation. Which some of them probably do.

Maybe we should be trying to forget her, Usha said. I wonder if everyone Evan knew has forgotten him. They've surely moved on anyway, graduated. Just like Usha will, and Lucas, and the rest of them, too. All my classmates will go on to college and jobs and families and lives. There won't be grief groups with remembrances. If they think of me, it'll only be once in a while, that poor girl who killed herself. And I'll still be here. In high school.

"I don't want them to think it," I admit, and my voice comes out so weak that I hate the sound of it, all desperate and wobbly. "I don't."

"Paige? What?"

"I don't want everyone to think I killed myself."

"I know," Evan says soothingly. "I know."

"No." I shake my head. "You don't know."

"What don't I know?"

"Usha said . . ." I have to make myself say it. "She said she wouldn't paint the memorial mural. She said she wasn't sad, she was angry. At me." My voice gets louder and shakier with each word, but I can't stop it. The tears are trapped in my dead body, just like I'm trapped here in this school. "She said that she wanted to forget me. And if my parents ever thought that I did this to myself, that I *wanted* this—"

"Paige," Evan repeats helplessly.

I wave him away, close my eyes, and take a few breaths. When I speak again, my voice is calm and certain. "They're *not* going to remember me like that. I'm going to find a way to change it."

"How?" Evan asks gently. "We can't talk to anyone, can't touch anything, can't *do* anything. What can you do?"

"I don't know yet," I tell him, "but something. I'll find a way to do something. I'm not going to end like this."

6: HOW I DIED

ON THE LAST DAY OF MY LIFE, I STOOD UNDER A LATE FEB-
ruary sky, the gray clouds pulled thin and high over our heads like a
veil. The sun was somewhere behind there, but I didn't know where.
Maybe if I scanned the sky slowly, I'd find a spot to the west where
the clouds burned white instead of gray, and that'd be the sun.
Otherwise, it was all sky, from top of head to soles of shoes, and we
were up there in it, because our physics teacher, Mr. Cochran, had
gotten permission to take us onto the roof for our egg-drop project.

We, the physics class, clumped at the center of the roof's flat,
cement slab, as far as possible from the foot-high lip around its
edge where Mr. Cochran stood. We shivered and stumbled against
each other, but we didn't break ranks. Mr. Cochran had been very
clear: he had a quiz ready. If there was any running, any pushing, any
"tomfoolery," we would march right down and take it.

"Let's not have you ending up like your eggs," he kept saying.

That afternoon, I was a good kid. We all were good kids, good
eggs. We stood at the center of the roof as we were told to. We didn't

run; we didn't push; we didn't tomfool. It's possible we whispered. It's possible we poked, and perhaps we turned to the roof's edge like how the bean plants in Mrs. Zimmer's biology room turned toward the dirty windows, even though they only opened inward, and then only a crack. I was alive then, though that wasn't something I thought about, because it wasn't remarkable; it just was.

"You were late again," Usha informed me, as if I didn't already know that. We stood as far from the rest of the group as we could without getting yelled at. Usha had fashioned her hair into a stiff egg-yolk mohawk in honor of our egg drop. It was the end of the day, though, and she'd started to smell like leftover breakfast.

"Headbang for me," I said to distract her, and she obliged, making a rocker scowl as she dipped her head. As soon as she'd finished, she went right back to "You were late yesterday. And twice last week." She poked a finger at my chest.

"Okay, okay, it's not a big deal. I forgot this." I held up my egg contraption. "I had to go back to my locker and get it."

"That took fifteen minutes?"

"I stopped to fix my hair. Not everyone has such a resilient hairstyle." I tweaked one of the peaks of her mohawk.

"True, true," Usha allowed, "but since when do you care about your hairstyle?"

The truth was, I hadn't been late because of homework or hair. I'd been late because I'd been waiting for Lucas Hayes in the burners' circle. After lunch, I'd found a note he'd left in my locker with a hastily drawn tree and a six, which meant to meet him in the burners' circle during sixth period, and I'd skipped American lit to do it. But he hadn't been there. No one had. I'd sat at the base of a tree for half an hour, scratching patterns in the dirt and staring up at the protective branches above me, before someone had finally arrived. And that someone hadn't been Lucas.

What are you even doing here, Wes Nolan? I thought when the sound of footsteps produced the cargo-jacketed, shaggy-haired burner. Wes was accompanied by Heath Mineo, the school drug dealer, so short and corrupt that he resembled a tiny mafia boss from the cartoons. Wes extracted a pack of cigarettes and tapped it against the trunk of one of the trees.

"Hey, look, it's Wheels!" Wes said.

I rolled my eyes.

"You know her?" Heath asked as if I weren't standing right there.

"Not even a little," I said at the same time Wes said, "A little."

"Someone stand you up?" Wes asked, flipping out two cigarettes and passing one to Heath.

I studied him for a moment, then dismissed him. There was no way he could know about Lucas and me. He was just trying to make a joke because when it came to Wes Nolan, everything was a joke.

Look at that. You're alone and friendless.

Ha.

Ha.

Ha.

"I'm just sitting here. That okay with you?"

"Free country," he said. "Free trees."

Wes and Heath smoked their cigarettes down in near silence while I returned to my dirt patterns, silently urging them to go, knowing that Lucas wouldn't show if they were here. But, maddeningly, when Heath finally dropped his butt in the mulch and left, Wes remained. I reached for my phone, but then brought my hand back. I didn't want Wes to see me checking the time.

"It's five minutes until the bell," he said, visibly pleased with himself. "So whoever you're meeting probably isn't going to come."

"I'm not meeting anyone." Instead of my phone, I took my egg-drop project out of my bag, unwrapping it from the sweater I'd used to cushion it.

Wes slid two more cigarettes out of the pack, offering one to me.

"I don't smoke."

"Why not? It gives you superpowers, you know."

"What? Like cancer?" I said, then grimaced. Everyone knew that Wes Nolan's dad had died of stomach cancer freshman year.

But if my comment bothered Wes, he didn't show it, saying, "Enough chemo, and you'll glow like a superhero." He tucked the cigarette back into the pack and nodded at my project. "What's in the box?"

"You want to hear about my physics homework?"

"I'm here smoking. You're here *not* smoking. Why not pass the time?"

"It's an egg drop."

"Like the soup?"

"Like you drop an egg off the roof, idiot," I said, and he grinned wider at the insult. "We had to create an enclosure for the egg using stuff from around the house, and today we're going to drop them from the school roof. If it doesn't break, you pass."

"And if it *does* break, you make egg-drop soup." He blew out a plume of smoke. "Can I see it?"

"Only if you promise not to pretend to drop it as a joke."

"You know me only too well, Paige Wheeler."

He turned the gift box around in his hands, studying its tiny springs (pilfered from three remote controls), peeking under the lid.

"How does it work?"

"The springs are hooked to a Ziploc bag full of shaving cream, and the egg is in the middle of the bag."

"Kind of a like an airbag in a car. Clever." Then, of course, he pretended to drop it.

"Does everything have to be a joke to you?"

He grinned. "Why not?"

"Because not everything's funny."

"What? Don't you like to laugh?"

"Of course. Who doesn't like to laugh?"

"You, maybe. You always scowl at me."

"Say something actually funny, and I'll laugh."

"Knock, knock," he said.

"Who's there?" I asked reluctantly.

"Me," he said.

"Me who?"

He grinned. "Just me."

"That's the joke?" I asked. "Knock, knock, who's there? Just me. That's not a joke. That's ridiculous."

"Ah, but you're laughing."

"Yeah. At its ridiculousness."

He was close enough that I could smell the cigarettes on him and, under that, another even smokier smell, like burnt leaves. One of his eyes was squintier than the other from the unevenness of his grin, but both eyes were the same warm brown. *If there's anyone whose smile would be asymmetrical*, I thought. But it must have been the kind of smile that made you want to smile back because that, I realized, was what I was doing.

I pulled away so quickly that my head clocked the tree trunk behind me. "Lucas helped me with it," I said, pointing to the project still in his hands.

"Lucas, huh?" Wes grunted, his smile dropping so fast I half expected to hear it shatter on the ground. "As in Lucas Hayes? As in the person you're *not* waiting for."

"I told you. I'm not meeting anyone."

Wes handed me back the box, then he flipped his cigarette onto the ground, stubbing it out with his heel, and walked to the edge of the burners' circle. But just before leaving, he turned around. "You know, if you were meeting me, I'd make a point of being here."

"And I'd make a point of losing track of time."

The grin was back, like I had complimented him instead of insulting him.

"Why are you smiling?" I asked.

"Because," he said, "that was funny." He tipped a salute and disappeared with the faint call of the school bell.

I'd waited another ten minutes for Lucas. He never came, and that, not hair or homework and definitely not Wes Nolan, was why I'd been late to physics.

Back on the roof, Usha's interrogation about my lateness was interrupted by a burst of talk from Kelsey and her ponies. The ponies were examining Kelsey's new piercing, a diamond stud in place of a beauty mark.

". . . brought a picture"—the wind caught Kelsey's voice—"so it'd be just like Marilyn's."

"Marilyn Manson's?" I said loudly.

Kelsey turned and wrinkled her nose. "No. Marilyn Monroe. The piercing artist said that I resemble her. Crazy, right?" The ponies circled up, probably to assure her that it wasn't crazy, not the slightest bit.

"Oh, that's right," I said to Usha. "Marilyn Monroe had a bunch of plastic surgery, too."

"Geez, Paige." Usha socked me in the arm. "Fight in your own weight class."

"Ugh. She thinks she's so edgy just because she broke up with Lucas Hayes and got a piercing at the mall."

"Meh. She's not that bad," Usha said. "Just kind of obvious."

"Usha Das!" Mr. Cochran called from the edge of the roof.

"She *is* that bad," I argued, "and then some more bad."

Usha shrugged then kissed my cheek with a smack before marching out to Mr. Cochran. Her contraption, which she held under one arm, was a cardboard replica of an old-fashioned plane, like the ones the Wright Brothers flew. It even had tiny paper-fastener propellers that spun. It must have taken hours to make, but it didn't meet any of the assignment criteria; it wouldn't protect her egg at all. Usha heaved it unceremoniously off the roof.

A giggle came from Kelsey and the ponies. It always sounded like they were laughing at you. I shot them a glare and accidentally met Kelsey's eyes, peering at me over the ponies' heads. Her eyes were wide and hazel and framed in flourishes of liner. I imagined Lucas gazing into those eyes. I looked down at the box in my hands, picturing the egg—perfect, white, seamless—in its center. I wondered what Usha would think if she knew I was hooking up with Kelsey's ex-boyfriend. I wondered what she'd think if she knew he'd stood me up.

No, I knew what she'd think of that.

"All right, Paige Wheeler!" Mr. Cochran called with a wave. Usha passed me on her way back and said happily, "Crash landing! Total yolk!"

The closer I got to the edge of the roof, the bigger the sky seemed, the smaller the roof. Even smaller, me. It must have shown on my face, because when I reached Mr. Cochran, he clapped a reassuring hand on my back. "You okay there?"

"Agoraphobia," I mumbled.

"You mean acrophobia."

"Right," I agreed, though really I'd meant agoraphobia. It wasn't that the building was too high, but that the sky was too *big*. The empty sky, my empty stomach, so big that I'd be lost in them. The parking lot was below, beyond it the road where shiny cars, not yet dimmed by the stipple of winter road salt, drove steadily to the strip mall or the on-ramp or the Gas-N-Go, and then home, always eventually home. I stepped a foot up onto the lip of the roof, testing my fear. My heart thunked; the sky stretched itself wider.

"Hey, now." Mr. Cochran clucked at my foot. "Feet on the ground."

His words were underscored by a squeal of hinges. Mr. Cochran and I both turned at the sound of a door swinging open. The rest of the class had turned, too, and was squinting at the shadowy figure in the doorway that led down to the school. I blinked, trying to see who it was. When he stepped out into the light and I saw who he was, I blinked again, this time from surprise.

"Lucas Hayes!" Mr. Cochran shouted. "What are you doing up here?"

Lucas looked past Mr. Cochran, his eyes snagging mine, which filled me with something more expansive than my fear of the roof, more encompassing than the cold sky. *He came here to see me.* A smile worked its way onto my lips. As soon as I realized, I yanked it off my face. I refused to beam dumbly at the boy who'd just stood me up. After all, I wasn't a no-respect burner girl. I wasn't poor, dead Brooke Lee.

"Coach C!" Lucas called. "I need you to sign this for me." He waved a paper in his hand and looked past me like I wasn't even there.

Suddenly it felt like it was true, that I *wasn't* there. And that made me feel embarrassed and resentful and tired, so completely tired that I wanted to lie down on the roof and stare out at the world with its toy cars, ribbon road, and twig trees. I turned away from Lucas and the rest of them, my arms still holding the egg contraption straight out into the big empty sky.

"Stay here," Mr. Cochran said to me, and I nodded. Where else would I go? Behind me, Mr. Cochran's voice faded as he started across the roof to sign Lucas's form. I looked down at my feet, the buckles of my boots dull under the hazy sky; one foot was still up on the roof's lip. And, almost as if I were watching myself do it, my other foot stepped up to join it. The horizon retreated an inch more, another row of houses now in my view. It was a victory over my fear, I decided. A victory of twelve inches, but a victory nonetheless. Suddenly I wasn't afraid anymore, not of the height, not the wide sky, not Kelsey Pope's whispers or Lucas's smile, which I could almost feel behind me, wedged between my shoulder blades.

"Lucas!" a boy's voice called. "Catch!"

And then the unmistakable sound of a cracking egg, followed by a gasp from my classmates.

"You were supposed to catch it!"

I started to turn around; I had the impulse to find Lucas's eyes again, sheepish from not having made the catch. Maybe this time our eyes would meet, and we would see each other, no more than a stretch of roof between us. But I must not have realized how close I was to the edge, because as I turned, my foot slipped. My stomach lurched; my breath filled my mouth in a phantom scream. Suddenly, I wasn't looking out at Lucas's eyes, but up at the sky, marbled and gray, no sun to be seen.

I'm falling, I said to myself. Or maybe someone else said it to me. My head hit the edge of the roof. My teeth bit together. My vision burst with a flash of pain so bright it could have been the sun, burning through that wispy sky.

7: SKETCHES OF BIRD AND GIRL

I WAKE UP WITH A GASP. FOR A SECOND, I DON'T KNOW WHERE I am. The light is all wrong; even in the darkest hour of the night, the glow of the streetlamp outside my bedroom comes through the slats of my blinds, dissecting my room into strips of shadow and light.

Then I remember that I'm not in my bedroom. I'm in the basement of the school, the dirt of the floor pressing against my check, the ghost frogs trilling around me. I must have fallen asleep in the library next to Evan and, once I'd stopped hovering, sunk through the floor all the way down to the basement. I'd dreamt I was falling, too, that dream everyone has where you wake up just before you hit the ground.

Well, *you* do. You wake up.

Me, I hit.

When I climb the stairs, the halls are filled and the tardy bell is clanging. People buzz by, some of them carry crumpled brown bags, others the neon-potion dregs of energy drinks. That's the bell for the end of lunch, then. I've slept through the whole morning.

With a gut-twist, I remember the day before: Kelsey starting the rumor, Lucas skipping my grief group, Usha refusing to paint the mural. This afternoon, the crowd still crawls with whispers of my name, the suicide rumor coughed from mouth to ear like a virus. I search the groups for Patient Zero and her flapping silk banner of hair. My eyes narrow when I spot it. Kelsey Pope. I follow her all the way to art class.

That I find Evan in the art room, hovering on the cupboards that line the back wall, is no surprise. He spends most of his day in the art room because, according to him, Mr. Fisk is the best teacher at Paul Revere High. But I'd forgotten that Usha has art this period, too. She stands at Mr. Fisk's desk with her sketchpad open. As Kelsey takes a seat with her ponies, I approach the front of the room apprehensively. Usha and I have only fought once, back in ninth grade. I don't remember what the fight was about, but I do remember that we didn't talk for a week. And, it felt exactly like this: angry and shameful and resentful and regretful all at once. At least Usha doesn't have her arms crossed over her chest today; at least she isn't talking in that horrible detached voice about how she wants to forget me.

"It's just . . ." She holds the book out and turns her head away, as if she can't bear to look at it. "It's just something I tried."

Birds.

She has drawn a flock of birds. The page is filled with them, gliding, flapping, and hovering. They are no birds I know, no robins, seagulls, egrets, or wrens. She has made up new breeds, new spreads of feather, new sequences of markings, new wingspans, bright eyes, scales, talons, crops, and crests. The style is cartoonlike, but not hasty, not comic; the shaft of each feather has been sketched out, the nostril of each beak. They are all in flight, these birds, and though there is no formation, no migration, their beaks all point in the same direction.

Usha has always been able to draw, turning an errant scribble in my notebook margin into a tiny monster or hothouse flower. When I'd watched her draw, it had seemed so easy—a mark like this here, a line like so there—but whenever I'd tried to re-create one of Usha's doodles myself, my monsters ended up smudgy blobs, my hothouse flowers, sticks. Usha would take the paper out of my clumsy hands and draw over it—a few quick lines, and suddenly my monster had charm, my flower had pollen and scent. I liked the fact that Usha could draw. In fact, I felt so fiercely proud of her that it was as if the talent were my own, as if there were something that special about me.

Mr. Fisk makes a few remarks about perspective—neither of them mentions yesterday's conversation about the mural—and I watch Usha retreat to her table, where she flips to a new page and begins to draw an ocean full of jellyfish.

I walk to Evan at the back of the room.

"Sleep well?" he asks with a grin.

"Thanks for waking me up before I sank through the floor," I tell him.

"Aw, but you looked so peaceful." Every once in a while, I get a peek past Evan's hall-monitor exterior, and what's beneath is pure infuriation. "What are you doing here?" he asks.

"Keeping an eye on her." I nod over at Kelsey, who's in a huddle with the other ponies, the light bouncing off their flat-ironed hair. "What do you think she'll say about me next?"

"Maybe nothing."

I give him a look.

"Maybe it just slipped out," he says. "Maybe she didn't mean to—"

Precisely then, a whisper of my name hisses from the pony table. "Hear that?"

"Hear what?" Evan asks.

"Over there. They just said my name."

"I didn't hear anything," Evan says. "They're not even talking. They're all looking at something." He squints. "What is that?"

It turns out to be a sketchbook, but the ponies are clustered so tightly around it that we can't even see the white of the page.

"I wasn't looking for it, I swear," one of them is saying, her voice chock-full of delight. "It was open in his cubby, like he'd left it that way on purpose. I couldn't *not* see it."

"And it's whose again?" Kelsey asks.

"You know, that one kid. Wes Nolan."

"Who?" Kelsey repeats.

"You know. That goofy stoner who sits over there."

"Oh, yeah," the other pony says. "Buy a new coat once a decade, you know?"

"And he drew all of these?" Kelsey asks.

"There are pages of them."

The girls are still blocking the sketchbook, which is just as well. I can already imagine the huge mammaries and drooling zombies Wes Nolan has been drawing. This has nothing to do with me, and I'm already turning away when Kelsey says, "Do you think she posed for these? She couldn't have, right?"

A girl posed for Wes Nolan's drawings?

"She must have," the pony with the book says. "He couldn't have drawn these all from memory."

"And I don't want to be mean," the other pony adds, "but who knows what she might have done? Right, Kelse?"

"Yeah. I guess."

"Who?" Evan says, trying to hop up to see and then land on the floor in a hover, with limited success.

The ponies fall silent. My mind isn't silent, though. It's packed with my own name, shouted in a roar that fills my ears. *Me. They're talking about me.* Then one of them shifts, and I can see it.

The edges of the paper are a cloud of blurred lead that clears in the paper's center to reveal a girl sitting at the base of a tree. She's slouched in a graceful curl, knees drawn to her chest. Her hair falls in a messy cascade of strands and shadows across a determined jaw and chin. There's a stick in her hand, and she's scratching designs in the dirt. Kelsey flips through the other pages, and there the girl is again and again. Always at the tree, always with a stick. In most of the sketches, she's looking down at the designs she's drawn, but in a few, her face is turned toward the viewer, her eyes wide and luminous, her lips bow-shaped and touched with a smile. She is much more delicate, more charming, much prettier than I ever could be. She is also, unmistakably, me.

I back away, all the way away, back to Usha's table and plant myself on an empty stool, Usha's pencil scratching next to me like a reassuring whisper. *My eyes hadn't met Wes's, not like that,* I think. *I hadn't been waiting there for* him. I'm angry, I realize. So angry I might start shouting.

At who? a small voice asks. *About what?*

At Wes of course, I think. *How dare he draw me like that!*

I pull in a breath and realize that I've been staring blindly at Usha's hand working across the page. She hasn't been drawing jellyfish, as I'd first thought, but parachutes. The domes are not made of translucent flesh, but panels of fabric. Not tentacles hanging down, but ropes, a curled skydiver dangling from each one. She's even drawn harnesses, the tiny buckles holding them to parachutes that lower them gently to the ground.

Evan arrives at my shoulder. "That was something."

"It was nothing," I say tersely.

But I look at the door, suddenly worried that Wes will bang through it, tardy as usual, with his stupid crooked grin and stupider jokes. I tell myself that it might not have even been me, the girl he drew. She hadn't even looked like me. Not really. I didn't have those eyes. Not that smile.

"Well, at least we found the *next* rumor about you," Evan says.

"You see how she is? Who knows what she might decide to say next."

"Actually, it was her friend who found—"

"The sick thing is she doesn't even know me. She knows nothing about me. She's just saying things for . . . I don't know why. Why do people say things like that?"

I shoot an evil look in the general direction of the ponies, but my eyes land on the table by the door. I hadn't seen it before, because it is small and situated in the corner and it holds only one student sitting by herself.

Greenvale Greene is looking right at me.

Our eyes lock. Hers are so light they're nearly colorless. Her clothes—the same jeans and hoodie as anyone else's—appear somehow ill-fitting and out of style, like wrinkled hand-me-downs. Her hair, lank and unbrushed, falls in her eyes.

Greenvale Greene, I think.

Paige Wheeler, a voice whispers in return.

I glance over my shoulder to see what Greenvale is really looking at, surely someone else behind me. But no one is there except for Evan and the blank wall. And when I turn back, Greenvale isn't there either. A flash of bony elbow, the sole of an off-brand shoe, and the door to the art room slams shut.

"Who was that?" Mr. Fisk looks up. "Who just left?"

"Harriet Greene," someone says. This is followed by a ripple of the word *Greenvale*, spoken almost as a superstition, like throwing salt over your shoulder or touching the points of the cross.

"Maybe she could ask for a hall pass next time," Fisk says.

"Maybe she really had to go," someone suggests, which elicits laughter.

I wonder if they'd still have laughed if they'd seen her face before she ran from the room. Eyes wide, mouth open in fear.

It was as if she'd seen a ghost.

8: THE RESISTANCE OF FALLING OBJECTS

"IT'S YOUR IMAGINATION," EVAN SAYS BEFORE I'VE EVEN FINISHED explaining. We stand in the hallway outside the art room, Greenvale nowhere in sight.

"It's not. She looked right at me."

"It's happened to me before, too," Evan explains. "You're just seeing what you want to see. You think they're looking at you, but really they're always looking at something else."

"Trust me. If I wanted someone to see me, it wouldn't be Greenvale Greene. Besides, there was nothing behind me, just the wall."

"Maybe she was looking at the wall." Evan tilts his head. "Who is this again?"

"You know, Greenvale Greene. She was sitting right by the door."

"I didn't see anyone by the door."

"I didn't see her at first either. She was practically in the corner.

She's pygmy-short, starvation-skinny, bangs in her face, huge eyes under the bangs."

He shakes his head, no recognition. "Is she a well-rounder or a biblical or—" I've taught Evan all of Usha's and my nicknames.

"No group. She's . . . well, she's crazy. Like, certified. Sophomore year she had some sort of breakdown and wouldn't leave her bedroom. Her parents sent her to a place . . . a facility or whatever you call it."

Evan adjusts the cuffs of his sweater so that they're even on his wrists. "Greenvale is a strange name."

"Her name isn't really Greenvale. Technically, it's Harriet. Greenvale is the name of the place where they sent her, and her last name is Greene, so everyone calls her Greenvale Greene." I frown. "Unfortunate coincidence, I guess."

Evan looks up from his sleeves. "If the place hadn't been named Greenvale, they would have come up with something else to call her."

I think of the nicknames Usha and I devised for our classmates with a tug of guilt. It wasn't the same, I tell myself, calling someone a well-rounder or a pony or a testo. Besides, I wouldn't have come up with the names if people didn't try so hard to fit in their tidy boxes. Except Greenvale, I realize. She didn't have a category, a group.

The bell rings, and the classroom doors pour out students. Evan and I back away from the crowds, but when Kelsey and the ponies pass us in a coltish, neighing herd, I start after them.

"Where are you going?" Evan calls.

I turn and shrug. "To hear what else she says about me."

I trail along behind the ponies, listening for Kelsey to mention my supposed suicide again. But the group is caught up in a debate about whether a comment one of their friends made at lunch was intended to be bitchy. All the way to the science hall, the debate rages on, and it isn't until we reach the classroom door that I remember what Kelsey has last period.

Physics. The class where I died.

I haven't been back here since that day. My old desk is still empty. The desks around it are empty, too, like the dead places in the ocean where the fish won't swim and the coral has turned all broken and gray. Mr. Cochran is still on extended leave, and the class starts perfunctorily with the substitute dropping a quiz on everyone's desk. Kelsey and the ponies dip their heads over their papers.

I wander the rows, pausing at Usha's desk. She marks the questions correctly until she gets to the last one, where she pauses, pencil hovering over the options.

Discounting air resistance, what is the increase in speed for each second an object falls?

I actually remember this one from our egg-drop study packet.

Answer A reads *15 feet/second^2*

Incorrect.

Answer C reads *56 feet/second^2*

Also incorrect.

Answer B reads *32 feet/second^2*

"Time," the sub calls. "Pencils down."

"It's B," I whisper to Usha. "Mark B."

Usha dips her pencil to circle C. Without thinking, I put my hand over hers, willing it to B. My hand should swipe right through her hand, her paper, the wood of the desk. But it doesn't; instead, it bumps against something. Or rather, something bumps against it. It's been so long since I've felt something like this, it takes me a moment to place it: resistance. It's a simple feeling, as if my hand has bumped into hers, but to me it's alien. I gape at my hand, then

Usha's. She hasn't marked the paper yet. In fact, she's stopped, pencil in midair, staring at the question like it's staring right back at her.

"Usha?" I say.

This time, I hear her answer me.

Paige.

I get a creeping sense of déjà vu. There'd been a similar whisper yesterday when Lucas and I stood at the edge of the road. What had happened exactly? Lucas had looked back at the burners' circle. I'd heard a whisper of my name, and then . . . On impulse, I reach out and put my hand through Usha's. Again, it bumps against something, but this time I push back, I push *through* it. I'm holding Usha's hand just like I did with Lucas's.

Then I realize that I'm not holding her hand at all. My hand *is* Usha's hand. *I'm holding her pencil.* I can feel the crimped wood of it, the keen edge of the paper under my other hand, the pebbly plastic of the chair beneath me, the firm tile of the floor resting under the soles of my shoes. I suck in a breath of surprise and feel even more surprise as I draw actual air into actual lungs.

I am Usha.

I move my hand (Usha's hand) and mark B.

I stare at the quiz, the trail of lead that I've left behind.

I'm bumped again. This time it's bigger than a bump; it's more like a rough shove, like when someone "unintentionally" plows into you in the hallway. I'm shoved out. Usha is above me, shaking her head foggily, and I'm not just shoved out; I'm sinking through the floor. I drop through the cottony insulation and sheathed electrical cords, through a government class set up like a mock court, through another floor that becomes a ceiling, another classroom flickering with the light of a projector, another floor, and then the basement, and a stack of old gymnastics mats that, comically, do nothing to break my fall. My legs drop through the mats, and I land at last, crouching on the dirt floor next to a croaking pair of ghost frogs.

As soon as I get my feet under me, I stand and race up the stairs, slamming my hovering boot soles down neatly on each step. I climb the next flight and the next and the next. Then it's down the hall and through the door into the physics classroom.

The sub ambles between the desks, sweeping up the last remaining quizzes. Usha's quiz is still on her desk, but he's headed to her now. I hurry forward, heedless of the desks that pass through my legs, focused only on the rectangle of white paper as if it's a beacon, a lit doorway through which I must pass.

I get there a moment before he does and glimpse the quiz paper just as he snatches it away.

I see it, though, the last answer.

Marked B.

9: NAMES

"DO YOU EVER HEAR PEOPLE SAY YOUR NAME?" I ASK BROOKE and Evan.

Mere feet away, the goalie paces from one end of the goal to the other. We're in the soccer goal, right inside where the ball is kicked, Brooke stretched out long, Evan and I crouched under the drape of the net. The field is bald but for a few stubborn patches of ashen snow. The team is shivering, sweatshirt sleeves pulled over their hands. I can feel it, too, the cold, but it doesn't chap or sting me. It's as if I'm only imagining what it feels like to be cold, as if I'm only saying the word *cold*. It's round in my mouth like a stone.

Shouts sail from the other end of the field, where the soccer ball dances between the feet of the eager players. I'm hoping the ball will stay over there. Brooke, however, likes it when the play comes this way. She rises and mimics the goalie's movements, shifting behind him. If a kick gets by, she'll pivot as if to catch the ball that he couldn't. But, of course, it just punches through her gut and socks into the net behind her.

"Do people talk about me?" Brooke says. "Yeah, all the time. They say, 'Brooke Lee is hanging around your boyfriend' or 'Brooke Lee has syphilis' or 'Brooke Lee is getting an abortion after school.'"

"I mean since you died."

"In that case, it's more like 'Brooke Lee traded hand jobs for cocaine' or 'Brooke Lee snorted lines off the bathroom floor.'"

I look away guiltily. Usha and I used to say things like that about Brooke. Everyone did. Though that's hardly a good defense.

"Do you mean *just* your name?" Evan asks. "Like someone is whispering it, but you don't know who?"

I sit up on my knees. "You've heard it, too?"

"I used to hear it. Down the hall or just behind me. *Evan, Evan.* Really quiet. Almost too quiet to hear." Brooke and I share a look. This is the most Evan has ever spoken about his death.

"Could you tell where it was coming from?"

"Not really. I heard it mostly right after I died, then less, then eventually it stopped. I haven't heard it in years." He looks away with a half shrug. "Honestly, I thought I'd gone crazy. Crazy enough to hear things, anyway." He looks at me. "But you hear it? Your name?"

"Sometimes," I say carefully. "One of the times, I thought it was Usha's voice." That's what it had sounded like, that moment during the physics quiz when I'd plunged my hand into hers. It was the same whisper that she'd leaned over, desk to desk, and poured into my ear during class hundreds of times before.

When I climbed back up to the physics classroom, I tried to repeat what I'd done, to slip back into Usha's body. I tried for the rest of the hour, but this time there wasn't a bump; there wasn't anything.

My hands passed through her like she wasn't even there, even though I knew it was me; I was the one who wasn't there.

I'd tried it with other people to see if that might work—up and down the rows, even the stupid sub, even Kelsey Pope. Nothing. When the final bell had rung, I'd walked out into the busiest intersection of the hallways and let them walk through me, all of them—well-rounders, biblicals, testos, burners, and the rest. The waves of people marched through me, and I'd tried to re-create the feeling I'd had with Usha of something fitting into place, a seat belt clicking, a deadbolt turning. But at the end of it, they were a procession of ghosts, and I was standing alone in an empty hallway.

I hadn't planned on hiding what had happened with Usha from the other dead kids until I found myself *not* telling them. But it was the right choice, I reassured myself. Brooke would have pestered me with questions, and Evan would have worried himself sick about the ramifications of it. And for what? Who even knew if I could do it again? I decided that I'd keep it to myself for now.

"Let me get this straight," Brooke says. "You think Usha is sitting around chanting your name?"

"She's not *chanting* my name," I explain. "It's like—"

"Like she's thinking it," Evan finishes, "and you can hear her thoughts."

"Yeah. Exactly. Like she's thinking it," I say. "You've never heard it?"

"Do I hear voices calling my name? No." But she rises and stands by the edge of the net, staring off into the field as if what we're saying has bothered her somehow.

The sun is almost gone now, its last few rays skating along the flat field. The soccer players amble off in twos and threes, balls kicked out ahead to chart their trajectory, the lines all meeting back at the school. The school building looks small from out here at the edge of the field, like you could jump off it and stand up on the ground with a *ta-da!*

"Did she say anything else?" Evan breaks into my reverie.

"Who?"

"Kelsey Pope. Did she say anything else about you?"

"No. I . . ." Inhabiting Usha had made me clean forget about Kelsey and the suicide rumor. But then a thought punches through me, strong and quick as the soccer ball through Brooke's gut: If I could mark Usha's quiz score, what else could I do? Could I walk around as her? Could I say things as her? Could I use Usha to tell people that the rumor isn't true?

I think of Evan's words in the library: *We can't talk to anyone, can't touch anything, can't change anything.* I smile because maybe now I can do all of those things.

10: THE TASTE OF SALT

THE NEXT MORNING, I MEET USHA IN THE STUDENT PARKING lot, noting that her old station wagon has a new dent in it. She has a punky black lace dress on and red rubber rain boots, even though it's far too chilly for rain. We head into the school, her breath a cloud in front of her face. I exhale nothing.

At the doors, one of the biblicals joins us, asking Usha how she's doing about ten times. I roll my eyes. The biblicals took no interest in Usha until I died, and now they practically want to baptize her. They're pleased, probably, that I supposedly killed myself; it gives them something to pray about. I'm so preoccupied with my thoughts that I've fallen back, so when Usha thinks my name and I lunge forward, my fingers just miss swiping her arm.

The next time Usha thinks of me doesn't come until late morning in her first art class—sculpture and pottery with Mr. Fisk—which means I can't take advantage of it then either. Since it's Fisk's class, that means Evan is perched on the low cupboard in the back of the room, and I'm forced to sit next to him like I've stopped by merely for the day's lesson.

The clock is a creeping sundial as Mr. Fisk spends most of the hour laboriously explaining glazing techniques. Even worse, he keeps dropping his marker, ducking to get it, then popping back up with a "Where was I?" before starting over at the beginning of the explanation.

"This is gripping," I say.

Evan's eyebrows shoot up. "You don't think he's a good teacher?"

"You sit in here day after day. I guess I thought he'd be amazing."

"Come on. He's not that bad."

That's when I hear it again—*Paige*—in Usha's whisper. She's doodling dragonflies on her notebook, their wings so huge that they spill over the margins, obscuring half her notes. I can't go near her, though, or Evan will see it. Which is precisely when he says, "I get why you're here."

"What do you mean?" I say. "Maybe I just like learning about glazing techniques."

He nods at Usha. "You want to know if she's thinking about you."

"Yeah, that's it," I say, and it sort of is.

"Well has she?" he asks.

"A couple of times."

"See?" Evan says. "She didn't forget you."

At lunch, people turn to look as Usha enters the cafeteria in her ridiculous red boots, but she glares at them and their faces spin away like targets in a carnival shooting gallery. I've never seen Usha narrow her eyes at people, much less outright glare at them; that was always me. Usha bypasses the table of biblicals who are waving her over and takes a spot at an empty table, yanking an orange, a sandwich, and chips out of her lunch sack. She sets them in a row, then goes straight for the chips, pulling apart the silvery lips of the bag. I stand directly behind her, hands at the ready, almost as if we were doing a trust fall.

"We saved you a seat," a voice chirps over my shoulder.

Two of the biblicals have appeared; they step past me and hover on either side of Usha. An angel on each shoulder. And a devil at her back. "You don't have to sit alone, you know."

Usha looks from one to the other of them. *Paige*, she thinks. This time the whisper has an annoyed quality, and I know why. The biblicals only want her to be friends with them because she's the school charity case, the girl whose only friend turned out to be a jumper. No wonder she wants everyone to forget me.

Sorry, Usha, but I won't be forgotten. I step between the two biblicals, plunging my hands, past any resistance, straight into Usha's back.

Salt.

Salt sharp on my tongue.

On Usha's tongue.

I close my mouth and let the salt taste spread out. I'm vaguely aware of the biblicals on either side of me, and the rest of the milk-slurping, sandwich-crust-balling cafeteria around us.

But at first there's nothing except for salt.

The taste is a shape: a prickly ball in my hands. The taste is a sound: a dozen taut wires plucked at once. The taste is a color: a gleaming silver. I bite down and feel the chips crunch, and that crunch is something else entirely. I chew, the bits of chip breaking apart on my teeth and tongue. It's been almost a month since I've eaten. I'd forgotten how it feels, how it tastes. Actually I'd forgotten taste existed altogether.

Then I see the orange sitting here in front of me. I grab it like it's a prize, which it is, bumpy and waxy and round and sour-sweet. I look down at my hands that are not my hands—light brown, knuckles whirled with charcoal, nails polished with picked-off green. I dig a painted finger into the orange peel and nearly laugh out loud at the feeling of pith caught under my nail. I dance my feet with a squeak, the rubber of the boots rubbing against each other. My squeak!

Then I remember that I'm in the middle of a crowded cafeteria. I'm Usha. So, as Usha, I should probably fight my impulse to run down the cafeteria line taking spoonfuls of all the foods. And maybe I shouldn't pass behind the tables of eaters, running my hands over my classmates' backs—the nubby flannels of the burners, the slick letterman leathers of the testos, and the careful cottons of the biblicals. I pull myself away from my salt and orange peel and squeaky boots. I am Usha. I have to act like Usha.

The biblicals have stopped hovering and have taken a seat on either side of me. Usha and I used to make fun of these girls, calling them by saints' names, which she'd pulled from an app on her phone: Agnes and Humbeline and Bertilia. But their real names are perfectly normal: Jenny, Erin, and Rachel.

I peel a strip off my orange and decide that I'm ready to try talking.

"Hey," I say. It works. The voice that comes out is Usha's. "I need to ask you something. As friends," I add for good measure.

"Of course you can," Jenny says.

"You've heard the rumors about Paige's death, right?" I ask. My question is accompanied by a faint stirring, a jostling inside me. *Is that you, Usha?* I wonder, setting my palms flat on the table. *I'm sorry, but I need you right now, just for a minute. Please don't push me out.* The stirring comes again. It's not nearly as strong as yesterday's shove, so I push back against it, focusing on being solid and still and here. It's sort of like hovering, like holding yourself in place.

The biblicals share a look, their bangs clean lines across their foreheads.

"Have you? Heard them?" I prod.

"No, I don't think so," one says in a tone that makes it clear she has.

"Really? You haven't heard that Paige committed—"

"We try not to gossip," Rachel cuts in.

"Okay, fine. But you have ears. People say she jumped. You heard that, right?"

"We heard it," Erin admits grimly. "Everyone's heard it."

"Well, I just want you to know—as a friend—that it's not true." Again comes the stirring feeling; this time, I ignore it.

The girls look at each other, then back at me.

"We hope it's not true," Rachel says.

"It's not," I say. "I was there. She fell."

"We hope so," Rachel repeats. "We pray for her."

I stare at her. She blinks back at me placidly.

"You *what*?"

"Pray for her," Rachel says uncertainly. She's heard something in my voice, something sharp-nailed, quick-tempered, and trapped in a small space. She continues, "If she killed herself, she can't go to heaven."

"What if there is no heaven?" I say.

"Pardon?"

"You know: tra-la-la heaven? What if it doesn't exist?"

The biblicals' smiles disappear, then reappear like cards in a magic trick.

"It's all right if you don't believe right now," Jenny says. "It takes time to—"

Enough of this. As if it isn't painful enough to be stuck here, stuck here forever, without having to hear this. I cut Jenny's sentence clean in half: "I don't believe or not believe. I *know*. I know, and I'll tell you so that you can know, too. Heaven doesn't exist. It's a story you've made up so that you can feel better about dying. But you know what? You die, and it's not better. It's just like it was before. Except worse because you're dead."

Suddenly I'm standing, with all of them staring up at me. The orange is squeezed in my palm, its sticky juice running down all the way to my wrist.

"It can be hard to understand His reasons—" Erin begins.

"You're not listening to me. There are no reasons. There is no Him, no pillows stuffed with fluffy clouds, no free harps at the door. No door. There isn't a heaven for you or for me. There's just this."

Their Chapsticked lips part in surprise. As I turn away from the table, I realize that half the cafeteria is staring at me. I stride past them and almost run smack into Kelsey Pope, who stands gawking at the recycling station with her empty tray. Her eyes widen, and she shuffles back, bumping into the bin.

"By the way," I say, "we *never* would have been friends." I drop the deflated orange at her feet and storm out of the cafeteria, my boots squeaking in anger with each step.

I end up in Brooke's bathroom, washing juice off my hand and arm. My anger has left as quickly as it came, and now I just feel empty and tired. And sticky. I glance into the mirror above the sink and meet the brown eyes of Usha's reflection. I make a face, feeling the skin and muscles pull into the shape I've told them to, but it's my expression on Usha's face, not her own.

That's when I realize my mistake: I've become one of the only people I want to talk to. Now Usha is further away than ever.

I wrap my arms around myself, feeling Usha's body, round arms, breasts, and stomach. It's pleasant, this extra flesh, as if it were here to comfort me. I shake my head, and Usha's bob swings against my cheeks and ears. I haven't worn my hair this short since I was little. I feel young and then, suddenly, very, very old.

You're only seventeen, I tell myself.

You're only seventeen forever, my self answers back.

I exhale. I hadn't expected to get so angry. I shouldn't have yelled at those biblicals. They weren't trying to hurt me. Maybe they'll leave Usha alone now anyway. That seemed to be what she'd wanted. *But she hadn't wanted it enough to yell at them,* I think guiltily. *That was you.*

Usha? I think as loud as I can. No answer, no stirring inside me, no shove. I wonder where she is now, if she saw the whole thing, hidden back there behind my eyes. Or maybe she's gone to sleep and will wake when I leave her. Forget that I don't even know how to leave her. Yesterday in physics, I'd only inhabited her for a second before I'd been pushed out again. As an experiment, I try to welcome it, the shove, but it doesn't come. My feet stay in Usha's red boots, planted firmly on the dirty tile. And I have to admit, I'm a little relieved that it didn't work, that I still have her body for at least a little while longer.

I flick water at my reflection in the mirror. It's all getting complicated. I'd been so focused on getting into Usha's body that I hadn't thought about what would happen after I was in it. And now I'd ruined my opportunity to stop the suicide rumor by making a scene. People would hardly believe Usha if she told them that my death wasn't a suicide, not now that she'd acted so crazy in front of the whole school.

"I'm sorry," I tell Usha's reflection, but the words come out in her voice, not mine. "I'm going to make it better."

But how? If only I could become more people, different people, then it'd be easy to reverse the gossip and set the record straight. To do that, though, I'd need more people to think about me more often. Or I'd need to predict when they'd think about me.

I stop.

I look in the mirror. Usha's face is smiling at me. I'm smiling at me. And I deserve it, this smile, because I've just had the best idea.

Mr. Fisk is in the middle of another glazing explanation when I show up in the doorway to his classroom. When he sees me lingering there, he signals for the class to pause, setting the lump of clay on the mat in front of him and walking to me while wiping earthy streaks onto his pants.

"Usha, what is it?"

"I'm sorry to interrupt."

"That's all right. You look flushed."

"I do?" I touch my cheeks.

"Are you okay?"

"Yeah. I'm okay. But . . ."

"Yes? You're okay?"

"I'm okay, but I've changed my mind."

"About what?"

"I want to paint the memorial mural." My words are answered with a shove so enormous that I nearly take a step back. I hold on tight, though, wrapping my arms around my body. (Usha's body.)

"You're sure?" Mr. Fisk asks.

"Completely." I nod emphatically. "I want to paint the mural. I want people to remember Paige."

II: PAINTING EYES

SMALL PROBLEM: I CAN'T PAINT.

During that afternoon's illustration class, Mr. Fisk has me wait by his desk while he gathers the mural materials. I wait for more resistance to come, but it doesn't. *I know you don't want to,* I tell Usha silently, *but you don't understand. Let me fix this, and you'll understand.*

Greenvale Greene sits quietly in her corner of the classroom. She doesn't look crazy today; she doesn't look at me at all. Wes Nolan is on time for once and bent over his sketchbook, drawing away. The ponies roll eyes at him and nicker. Kelsey, though, seems more concerned with stealing worried glances at me. I must've scared her in the cafeteria. Good. The pony next to Kelsey whispers something and nods at Wes. Is he drawing me again? I wander to the window by Wes's table and try to peek over his shoulder. I'm not used to casting shadows, though, and when I lean over, he immediately looks up.

"Eyes on your own paper, Das," he says with a grin. As usual, everything's a joke. Too bad death isn't that funny, Wes Nolan.

"Sorry," I mutter. "Just curious."

"Oh, this?" He flashes the page. "Bowl of fruit."

And that's just what it is, the grapes at odd angles on their vine, the orange a little lumpy. It's not a picture of me after all. A relief, of course, and never mind that twinge of disappointment. It's just that when I close my eyes, she's painted on the backs of my lids, that girl he drew, the branches of her tree spread out above her. I thought if maybe I saw her one more time, I could get her out of my head.

"I don't even like to eat fruit, much less draw it," Wes grumbles.

"What do you like to draw?" I ask, then think, *Duh. You.* And I wish I could unask the question.

Wes answers, "People."

"Just . . . just anyone?"

He thinks for a moment. "Anyone who sticks in my mind."

"Oh," I say, not sure if I'm relieved or disappointed. *What is it?* I want to ask him. *What is it that makes someone stick in your mind?*

"Usha," Mr. Fisk calls me from the doorway. I turn, but Wes calls me back. "Hey, are you painting that mural? For Wheels?" *Paige,* his mind whispers.

"Who?" I ask belligerently.

"For Paige," he says.

"Yeah," I say cautiously. "Why?"

"No reason." He shrugs, crooked shoulders, crooked smile. "Just . . . I'll look forward to seeing it when it's done."

Mr. Fisk takes me to the blank stretch of wall by the doors to the student parking lot. He sets me up with a ladder, a drop cloth, cans of paint, and brushes. He reminds me that Principal Bosworth has given me creative control, but with the understanding that he, Mr. Fisk, is overseeing the project. "No pressure," he says. "Just let me know when you have some of it up on the wall." He also rolls out an overhead projector, in case I want to draw the design first and project it onto the wall to trace over with paint. I definitely don't want to do this, as it would make it immediately obvious that I have no idea what I'm doing. Instead, I content myself with dipping the brushes in and out of the paint cans and staring at the wall. I tell myself that Usha is here with me. She's here, and she'll guide my hand.

I stare at my hand.

It doesn't move.

After half an hour, I have succeeded in creating two eyes, or at least two ovalish shapes that I intend to be eyes: one oval is a little higher than the other, and both of them leak drips of paint. I try to make them like the eyes in Wes's sketchbook—round, dark, glimmering with humor and life. Half a can of paint, three different brushes, and numerous drips on the drop cloth later, I'm proud to say that they look exactly like uneven, blobby black ovals.

People pass by as I paint, pausing for a moment to watch. Though none of them speak to me, all of their minds whisper my name. I grin. It's already working.

Brooke and Evan show up near the end of the hour. I'm careful to let my gaze pass over them like I can't see them. For a moment, I worry that they'll be able to see me, Paige, standing here plain as can be in Usha's clothing. Or maybe I'll appear as a misty apparition, smothering Usha in a Paige-shaped fog.

"So this is it?" Brooke asks archly. "That chick better not paint me fat."

"Paige should see this," Evan says.

"Paige should see two mucky dots of black paint?"

"Yeah, let's find her."

"Oh, yes. Let's hurry," Brooke says sarcastically.

"Come on," Evan cajoles. "Even if she pretends to be all tough, this will make her totally happy."

On the ladder, my brush pauses. *I don't do that,* I think, annoyed.

But Brooke snorts laughter. "Want to make a bet about how many times she shrugs and says, 'I don't care'?"

"I bet five times," Evan says.

"Fine. I bet six."

"That's cheap," Evan says, "betting one over mine."

"That's how the game is played, mister," Brooke replies. Then there's silence, and I'm about to turn around to see if they're still there when Brooke speaks again. "Do you think there will ever be a time when we don't care? When this—here, now—is our new life? And what came before was just . . . before?"

"I hope not," Evan says.

"Why? Don't you want to forget about all that?"

"It was my life," he says simply.

"I'd forget it all if I could," Brooke says, "but then they gotta go and paint a damn mural to remind me."

"I don't know," Evan says as they walk away. "I think a mural might be kind of nice. Think of it. Something there just for you."

After they leave, I climb down off the ladder and paint something tiny, right by the baseboard. Sure it's still a little blobby and uneven, but it's recognizably a moth. A miniature secret moth, something there just for Evan.

That's when Lucas Hayes marches past, telltale gold pass in his hand. He doesn't think my name; he's too busy glancing over his shoulder to even notice the mural or me, crouched behind my ladder. I expect to see his requisite group of testos following behind as if the coach has ordered them to practice formation even as they walk down the hall. But when Lucas glances over his shoulder once more, I realize that he's not waiting for his friends, but rather making sure that no one is following him.

Which is when I decide to do just that.

. . .

The girls' bathroom in the hall outside the gym is pristine. No knots of shed hair on the floor, no lipstick kisses on the mirror, or soap grime in the sink basins. Even the tile looks new here, its grout bright white, although it's years old.

Why so clean?

No one uses it.

If you're near the gym and you have to go, you use the bathrooms in the locker room or you backtrack to the one near the art room because, despite appearances, this bathroom isn't a bathroom. It's a trading depot. What's traded here? A variety of goods and services: cigarettes, pot, soda bottles half-drained and refilled with booze, gropes, cheat sheets, gossip, swirlies, clothing ensembles, fake IDs, burner saliva and (it's rumored) other bodily fluids, forged hall passes, reputations, and, this past September, a girl's life.

Since Brooke's death, most kids skirt the bathroom, though a few still linger when they pass, as if the door might swing open, revealing some whirling vortex, some forbidden fruit, a crimson-skinned secret of mortality offered just to them.

I follow Lucas at a distance, watching him walk into the girls' bathroom without breaking his stride. After counting to ten, with pulse pounding, I follow him in. Thankfully, the tiled entryway is empty. Two voices float from around the corner, where the sinks and stalls are.

". . . have to choose here?" Lucas says.

"But this is the best spot," the other voice says. A guy. He sounds familiar, but I can't place him. "Everyone thinks it's creepy, so they don't come here."

"I'd rather not come here either."

"That's new."

"No it's not," Lucas says in a dangerous tone. "You think I like coming back here?"

"Calm down. Let's just do it and you can leave."

Then, a rustling, and I can barely keep myself from peeking around the corner to see what they're doing. But I can't. I've already embarrassed Usha with the scene in the cafeteria; I won't have her blunder into God-knows-what secret meeting. Then I realize I don't have to blunder anywhere. If I sneak out, back into the hallway, eventually Lucas and the mystery guy will leave the bathroom, and I'll see them when they do.

Back in the hall, I post myself by the trophy case across from the bathroom and stare at it as if I'm actually interested in these lumps of metal earned for jumping high, bouncing a rubber ball, or knocking some poor sucker unconscious. What I'm really interested in is the reflection in the glass case of the bathroom door behind me. In fact, I'm concentrating so hard on that door that I jump when I hear the whisper.

"Usha?" a tiny voice says.

Greenvale Greene stands just next to me. Even though she's come from art class, she's still in her gym clothes—an oversized Paul Revere sweatshirt and shorts that pull into a tight V over her crotch. The paddle of Mr. Fisk's bathroom pass is pressed against her thigh, which is so pale that I can see the marbling of blue veins underneath the skin.

"You weren't by the mural," she says, her voice phlegmy, as if she hasn't spoken yet today.

"I took a walk. For inspiration."

"All that paint is still there." She fidgets. "You might want to put it away before someone pours it over the wall or floor or something."

"I don't think anyone would do that."

"You don't?"

"It's a memorial mural, so vandalizing it would be pretty harsh."

"Oh. I guess so." She pulls at the hem of her shorts, not that the extra quarter inch covers much of her stick legs.

I wait patiently for her to leave. She's odd and, well, exasperating. No wonder people make fun of her. Why is she standing silent and fidgeting? Why not head on her way?

Finally she says, "I'm sorry about your friend."

"Thanks," I say; then, on impulse, "what happened to your regular clothes?"

She looks down at her gym clothes as if she's only just realized she's wearing them. "Oh," she says. "The toilet."

"The, um, what?"

"Someone put them in the toilet while I was in gym class."

"That's awful."

She sways in place. "I guess. After the last time it happened, I started keeping a spare set of gym clothes in my locker. See?" She plucks at the armpit of her sweatshirt, pulling the fabric up toward my face. "Freshly washed. Doesn't smell."

"That's okay." I pull back. "I believe you."

When I step back, Greenvale takes my place and breathes on the streak of grease my fingers have left, lifting her sweatshirted hand to rub the glass clean.

"Why bother?" I ask.

"Oh." She gestures at the gold and silver cups. "I think they're pretty. I mean, imagine doing something like that."

For a moment, I try to imagine it—the globe of the ball between my hands, the ribbon breaking across my chest, the faraway roar from the stands—and maybe she's right. Maybe it is something to imagine. But then I notice the reflection in the glass.

The bathroom door. I haven't been watching it.

"Excuse me," I say, leaving Greenvale by the trophy case.

But when I push open the bathroom door, it's too late. The bathroom is empty. Lucas Hayes and whoever he was meeting are long gone.

Mr. Fisk has asked me to tape a sheet over the mural at the end of each day so that no one can see my (ahem) progress until I'm completely done. Honestly, I'm happy to cover up my blobby ovals. Besides, everyone will know why the sheet is up there anyway. As they pass, they won't be able to help thinking of me. I'll have my pick of them. I sit through physics, planning what I'll do tomorrow, how I can undo the rumor of my suicide.

After the final bell rings, I make it halfway to the parking lot before I stop abruptly in the center of the hallway, a stone in the middle of a rushing river. Everyone is leaving for the day. It hits me that, today, maybe I can leave, too. I ignore Usha's station wagon parked in the last row of the lot. I'm not sure what will happen when I cross the property line, so I'd rather not be driving a car. Usha's coat has pockets, and I ignore them, too, enjoying the sting of the early spring air on my skin. The road just ahead of me looks like a dark river with banks of frost-stiff grass. *The Lethe*, I think, wondering what coin I will have to pay to cross its waters.

As I'm walking, I'm remembering how when I'd come home, the steam from the kitchen would puff out to greet me only a second before my mother's voice, calling, *Paige? That you, honey?* Then at dinner, my parents and I would go around the table in turn, each of us sharing one event from our day. It had to be something tiny, like eating a different type of bread for lunch or seeing a strangely marked cat on a windowsill. *Today*, I could say, *I came home after school. Today I came home.* I'm walking faster across the lot, and then I'm running toward the road, running *onto* it, running, running home, running—

Off the ledge of the roof.

The momentum is still in my body, but before it can carry me forward, I crouch down and grab the lip of the roof, holding myself teetering on the brink of the building. It was too much to hope that I could leave. And yet I'd let myself hope it. I should have known that it'd be just like before, that the school wouldn't let me go, that it'd pick me up and set me back down on my death spot.

My hands, when I look down at them, are my own—nails clipped straight across, star-shaped scar on one knuckle, opal ring inherited from my grandmother. I am me again. I cling to that little square of cement, feeling the rough of it under my palms, the only thing I can feel. The second I step off this square of cement, I'll be insubstantial again—no dark green front door, no steam on my cheeks, no voice calling from the kitchen, no cat, no bread. My hands won't even be cold anymore, because they aren't really hands. I press my palms against my eyes.

When I lower my hands, I'm looking out across the parking lot, its car roofs laid out like tarot cards on a table. Past the cars, a chubby Indian girl in red rubber boots walks determinedly across the road where I can't go. She sinks down in her wool coat, letting it shield her from the wind. She wears no gloves, and her hands are pink from the cold. After a moment, she raises her hands to her mouth, blowing hot breath before shoving them into her pockets to keep them warm.

12: SOME GIRL WHO DIED

THE MEMORIAL MURAL WORKS JUST AS I'D HOPED IT WOULD.
The next morning, I stand under it as the crowds come in from the
parking lot. Almost everyone glances at the white sheet fastened to
the wall as they pass it, and my name is whispered in the voices of a
dozen different minds. Brooke and Evan stand with me.

"I hear it," Brooke says, her eyes closed and her chin tipped up
as if she has found a sunbeam to bask in. She opens her eyes. "You're
right. I've heard it before. I just didn't know to listen for it. It's them
thinking of me. It's . . ." She shakes her head.

"That's great!" Evan says, overly cheery.

"You don't hear anything?" I ask him.

"None of them knew me. How could they remember me?"

I think about that, being forgotten, being lost to time. That'll be
me someday, just like Evan. It'll be them, too, all of them bustling
by. Someday they'll die and be forgotten. They just get a little longer
to ignore the fact.

"It's nice, though, right?" Evan continues, his voice scrubbed bright and shiny. "So many people thinking about you?"

"That all depends on what they're thinking," Brooke says.

He turns to me. "And Usha is painting the mural after all?"

"Yup," I say. "She is."

I wonder, nervously, if Usha would agree with that statement. I've been waiting for her since last night, the questions burning inside me: Does she remember asking Fisk to paint the mural? Does she remember any of it? The fight with the biblicals? The mysterious Lucas meeting? The conversation with Greenvale? I lived an entire afternoon of Usha's life. *Stole it from her*, a rude little corner of my mind chides. Usha will have plenty of afternoons, I tell the corner. She can spare one of them.

When Usha finally arrives, I follow her to her locker and am surprised to find one of the biblicals, Jenny, waiting there wearing a stiff smile. Usha eyes her warily.

Shit, I think. *I'm caught.*

But then I realize that this is perfect. Surely, Jenny will talk about what happened in the cafeteria yesterday. And by Usha's reaction, I can figure out what she remembers from when I was inhabiting her.

Jenny clicks her heels together smartly like a secretary on a TV show. "I want to apologize. For yesterday."

Usha turns to her locker, dialing the lock in three quick moves, opening it with a fourth. "Why are you apologizing?" she says quietly, and my stomach lurches. Does she not remember any of it? Was the entire afternoon a blank? Did she close her eyes in the cafeteria and open them again, hours later, at the edge of school grounds? She must think she's going crazy, losing time like that. Will she tell her parents or Mrs. Morello? Will they send her to the Greenvale facility like Greenvale Greene?

But then I realize over the whirr of my panicked thoughts that Usha is still talking. "If anyone apologizes, it should be me," she tells Jenny. "I'm the one who yelled at you." She bites her lip. "I don't know why I yelled like that. I guess I lost my temper. I didn't used to get angry, but it seems like I'm yelling at everyone these days. I'm sorry anyway."

"No. You don't need to . . . Don't apologize. I had no right to start preaching about that stuff." Jenny touches her fingers to the slats of the locker next to Usha's. "I shouldn't . . . not everyone believes . . ."

"But it's a nice thing to believe." Usha moves her bag from one shoulder to the other, gives the locker dial another spin without even looking at the numbers. "Sometimes I wish I could believe in something like that."

"But you don't have to . . . not to be friends with us."

"Friends with you?" Usha's mouth twists, and Jenny blushes.

She stammers, "I didn't mean to assume. . . . That was a stupid thing to—"

"No. Hey. You can say that . . . you can . . . We could be friends." She pauses. "But . . ."

"What?" Jenny says. "You can tell me."

"You only wanted to be friends with me because of Paige." *Paige*, her mind echoes. "I mean, didn't you?"

"Oh." Jenny moves her hand from the locker to her chest, a parody of surprise. It's so broad, it's almost like an impression of the biblicals that Usha or I would have done. Except, I realize, there's no sarcasm there. Jenny means it. She means everything she says.

And this time Usha's not laughing.

"Is that what you thought?" Jenny asks.

"It seemed like—"

"No, I know." Jenny clasps her hands in front of her like a pleading silent-movie heroine, and again it's obvious that she means this gesture sincerely. "After . . . what happened . . . we thought you could use someone to sit with at lunch. So, that was because of Paige, I guess. But that's not why you're our friend."

"Why, then?"

"We like you. That's all."

"Okay." Usha smiles her smile. "That's okay, then."

After Usha and Jenny head off to class, I sit at the base of Usha's locker. This is how it will be now, I tell myself. Usha will have a new best friend. Lucas will have a new not-girlfriend. Everyone else will have their shocking suicide story. I'll have some dried paint on a wall. Unless . . .

I go over the girls' conversation in my head, weighing each sentence. Usha apologized for yelling at the biblicals. Could this be how it works? Not only does she remember everything I did yesterday, but from what she said, she accepts the actions as her own. She didn't black out. She wasn't watching me from behind her eyes. She wasn't consciously trying to push me out of her body. I was her, and she was me. And if this is true, it means that I can be anyone, do anything.

When I return to the mural, the hallway is empty. The late bell has rung, and Brooke and Evan have moved on to their various time fillers—Evan to class, Brooke to wander. I still haven't told them about my ability to inhabit people. *Soon,* I promise guiltily.

I startle as the school door slams open, barely regaining my hover when I hit the ground again. A good fifteen minutes after the tardy bell, and Lucas Hayes has arrived. Even though he's late, he doesn't hurry. Why bother? He has a pack of blank hall passes in his bag, the perk of being basketball captain. Lucas Hayes. My secret . . . something. Kelsey Pope's very public ex-boyfriend.

And yes, I want to fix the rumor about my death. And yes, last night, I thought up a dozen different ways to do that. But first, there's something I have to do, something I've always wanted to know. I want to know how Lucas Hayes really felt about me.

Inhabiting Usha's body was one thing; inhabiting one of the testos' bodies is a million things. I choose the least sweaty, least beefy of Lucas's friends: lanky, shy Joe Schultz, who happens to pause by the mural on his way to the gym. Joe is so quiet, I don't know that I've ever heard him talk before, so it's strange to hear my name whispered in the deep, rumbling voice of his thoughts. Though it's not nearly as strange as his body.

Usha and I had been best friends since middle school. We'd shared clothing, locker rooms, beds at slumber parties. Usha's body was as familiar as another person's body could be. Even so, it was little preparation for suddenly being her—different heights, different weights, different muscles pulling different bones. Essentially, different physics equations.

But, being Joe . . .

How can I describe it? If Usha's body was a favorite pair of jeans, Joe's is a Halloween costume.

For one thing, he's a guy with, um, all the guy features. I try to avoid thinking about the soft, swinging weight between my legs, which forces me to adjust the width and roll of my steps. Also now, suddenly, I'm a good six inches taller, with long limbs and ropy muscles. Joe is an athlete, tall, fast, and strong. I can feel that just walking down the hall, the potential for power and speed. I have the impulse to double back to the gym and dunk a basketball like some stupid testo.

Instead, I head to the locker banks where I find Lucas and the testos in a cluster. I stand uncertainly at their backs, afraid to actually speak. I don't know how to be a guy, much less a testo sort of guy. They'll know. They'll know right away. But then, one of them says, "Hey, Schultz." And when I realize that he means me, I say, "Hey" back, and they shuffle aside to make room for me.

I expected the testos to be talking about free throws or girls' tits or something, but in fact, they're talking about Mr. Cochran and how he hasn't yet returned from his leave.

"We should get a group of guys from the team and go over to his house," Brian Mulligan is saying.

"I'll go," Chad Harp offers. "It'd suck to be sitting there thinking that you caused some girl's death." Their minds whisper my name.

"That's what I mean," Brian says. "He should know what people are saying. He should know that it wasn't his fault."

"Maybe it was his fault," Lucas says softly.

The boys shift and look at each other nervously. I watch Lucas. The usual confidence is gone from his eyes. Today, he doesn't look like the world is his birthday present; he doesn't look like he even has a birthday.

"But, Luke, if that girl wanted to jump, what could he have done?"

"I don't know." Lucas scratches the back of his neck, studying the floor tiles. "But he was the teacher. Maybe he should have done something. Maybe he shouldn't have walked away."

Then there's a pause. I take a breath, take a chance. "What if she *didn't* jump?"

They all look at me with vague surprise. I wonder, belatedly, how often Joe speaks, much less speaks about gossip. He doesn't seem like much of a presence; in fact, he didn't offer any push-back when I inhabited him.

"Naw, dude. She jumped." Brian slaps his hand flat on the locker for emphasis. "It's all around the entire school."

"But that's just gossip," I say.

"I heard that people *saw* her jump," Chad says.

"Exactly." Brian slaps the locker again. "There was a whole roof full of people."

"You were there on the roof," I say to Lucas, Joe's heart suddenly pounding in his chest as I wait for Lucas's answer. "Did you see it?"

"I was talking to Coach C," he says, looking away.

"So you didn't see it, then?" I press, half hopeful that he did, so that he can tell these guys how I didn't jump, half relieved that he didn't, because how awful to see someone die, someone you knew, someone you'd kissed. I touch a thumb to my lips. Joe's lips. They're chapped, my thumb rubbing against little flakes of peeling skin.

"I didn't see it," Lucas confirms, pulling the hood of his sweatshirt up around his neck. "Greg O. threw me his egg thing, that project they were doing, and it splattered. I was looking at that, everyone was. Then some girl screamed. And when I looked up again, the ledge was empty. She'd been right there a second ago, then she . . . wasn't."

His voice is thin, guarded. The same voice as when I'd said he'd practically saved a girl's life. *Don't say that. I didn't save her.* And it strikes me that Lucas was there for both Brooke's death and mine, and both times a second too late.

"That's rough," one of the guys says.

"First Brooke Lee, then Paige Wheeler," someone adds, giving voice to my exact thoughts.

"Yeah, Hayes, why you gotta go around killing all the girls at our school?" another says, and the guys laugh darkly at this, until they realize that Lucas and I aren't laughing along with them.

"You knew her, right?" I ask.

Lucas looks up at me, eyes flashing. "What?"

"Paige Wheeler. I heard . . . you knew her."

Lucas presses his lips together, for a moment, the fear plain on his face. He drops his head, and when he looks up again, the fear is gone and his confidence is back.

"Not really," he says smoothly.

I suddenly feel more solid than ever, solider than Joe, solider than flesh and bone. I feel like I'm made of stone and will never move again, not even a twitch.

"Not even a little bit?" I ask.

"Naw. She was just some girl," Lucas says. "Some girl who died."

I get away from the testos as quickly as I can. I want to stop this inhabitation; I wait for Joe to push me out, but he doesn't. I'm stuck. Finally, I tell the hall monitor that I left my homework in my car, then I walk out all the way to the property line, stepping across it. From the edge of the roof, I look down to see what Joe will do. He stands there for a moment, like he's walked into a room but forgotten what he meant to get there, then he shakes his head and turns back to the school.

Me, I feel like the object that's been forgotten. I feel like the act of forgetting. When I felt this way before, I would go to Usha, who'd drag me out to her car, where she would play the right music (screamy) at the right volume (loud) and drive the right speed (fast). We would fly down those roads. Just fly.

Now I have no music, no car, no roads. No Usha. No flying.

But I do have Evan.

I take a seat next to him on the cupboards in the back of Fisk's room. Evan must sense that something is wrong, but he doesn't ask me anything. I know that I've only lived a short life and an even shorter afterlife, but I think I can say that this is a rare quality. Usha had it. Lucas, too, actually. The bastard.

Evan and I sit in silence until the class break, when I turn to him and say, "Apparently, I'm just some girl who died."

"Who made that lovely remark?"

"Lucas Hayes."

Evan squints. "And you care what Lucas Hayes says since . . . ?"

"Since I was hooking up with him." I throw my hands up. "Now you know."

Evan raises his eyebrows. "Oh. When were—?"

"From December until dead. Just a few months."

"I'm sorry, I didn't—"

"Of course you didn't know. No one knew. Because it was no big deal. Just a thing. A weird thing. So that's it. So there." I brush my hands together, done with it. Done with Lucas. I eye Evan. "So, Brooke didn't tell you about Lucas and me?"

"She knew?"

"She was the only one who knew. She saw us."

"No, she didn't tell me."

"But you don't seem that surprised."

He smiles briefly and unhappily. "It's a familiar situation."

"Is it? Not for me. Not that it matters. I mean, technically, he's right. Technically that's who I am: some girl who died."

"That's not who you are."

We sit in silence again.

"Did you like him?" Evan asks.

"No. A little. He was nice. When we were alone, he was nice."

"He's a coward, though," Evan says.

"Do you know him?"

"I know cowards."

"Yeah, I guess he is." I sigh.

I look to Evan, but he isn't looking at me anymore. His gaze is at the front of the room, where Mr. Fisk sweeps a long arm, erasing the board.

13: I AM EVERYONE

OVER THE NEXT COUPLE OF WEEKS, I LURK BY THE MURAL, covered in a sheet like old furniture, waiting for someone to pass and think of me, which someone always eventually does. Then, quick as a whisper, I'm in their skin. I am everyone. I'm a burner, a testo, a biblical, a well-rounder, a nobody. Most of all, I am alive.

With every new inhabitation, I hang around the person's group of friends. I say as little as possible so that I don't give myself away, and even still sometimes I say the wrong thing, and they all turn and look at me funny. But it's not like they could ever guess the truth. It's not like they could know who I really am. And when I can, I guide the conversation to poor Paige Wheeler's suicide, poor dead Paige.

My lines are simple: "That's such a lie. Kelsey Pope just wants attention. You know how girls like her are." Most groups agree with me immediately and shake their heads at the duplicity of spoiled, self-centered Kelsey Pope. A scant few argue that no one would lie about something so terrible, especially not Kelsey, who's really sweet if you get to know her. Once I'm out, I listen carefully for the suicide rumor to snuff out. But it is stubborn. Unlike me, it lives on.

Every day at lunch, I inhabit Jenny, Usha's new best friend. We don't sit and eat at Usha's locker, like she and I used to, but in the cafeteria with the other biblicals.

"Do you ever wonder what Paige would think of this?" I say to the table one afternoon. "If she were here?"

"Like her spirit?" Erin asks. "Like, looking down at us?"

"More like just here, invisible in the school."

"What movies have you been watching?" The biblicals laugh and gently shake their heads.

"But there's purgatory, right?" I ask them. "That's in the Bible."

Usha looks up from her lunch. "You're saying that high school could be a kind of purgatory?"

"Or hell," one of the biblicals says.

"Hell for sure," another agrees.

"No, it's purgatory," Usha maintains. "Think about it. We're all here waiting, right? Waiting to move on, to find out what's next."

"Yeah, exactly," I say, and she looks over at me. There's something in my tone that I didn't intend. Something like longing.

I spot Lucas across the cafeteria at a table thick with ponies and testos. He's laughing at something, the sound of it bright and open, his eyes in crinkles. But today, his laughter doesn't charm me. It's like watching the levels of music on a synthesizer instead of listening to music itself. I hear his voice again: *She was just some girl who died.*

I suddenly regret not telling Usha about Lucas and me. She wouldn't have laughed at me for liking a testo. And she wouldn't have told anyone if I'd asked her not to. Though she would have asked *me* why it had to be a secret, and she would have known that it was Lucas's secret, not mine. Thinking about what Usha would have said allows me to admit the truth to myself: I would've walked down the hall with Lucas, sat with him at lunch, put on the dress and gone to prom, all that stupid stuff. He just never asked.

"Hey," Usha says, giving my sleeve a tug.

"Sorry," I say. "Distracted."

"Me, too." Usha smiles. "Like about ninety-nine percent of the time."

I smile back.

"That rumor about Paige?" I say. "You were right. I don't believe it."

Usha's smile shrinks up. "I was right?"

"Yeah. A couple of weeks ago, when you told us that it wasn't true? You were right."

Usha sighs. "Look. I was just . . . saying things. I don't . . . I don't know."

"But Paige was your friend, right?"

She crosses her arms over her chest, not like she's hugging herself, but like she's holding herself together. "She was."

"So you don't think she'd—"

"I don't want to talk about it," Usha says firmly.

"Okay, but you know that Kelsey Pope was probably just trying to get attention and be dramatic, right? I mean, it's just a stupid rumor."

"It's . . ." Usha picks at her orange.

"It's what?" I prompt. "Usha?"

Usha looks up. "Kelsey shouldn't have said it. Now can we *please* talk about anything else?"

I feel a twinge of anger mixed in among the stew of desperation and loss. Usha had told Mr. Fisk that I was supposed to be her friend, but Usha was supposed to be my friend, too. So why would she believe the worst about me?

After lunch, I walk Jenny out to the property line and hurry to the art room in time to inhabit Usha for another session of mural painting. This attempt at painting doesn't go any better than our other sessions, but I'm afraid *not* to inhabit her. She didn't want to paint the thing in the first place; she could very easily tell Mr. Fisk that she's going to quit. So, I get up on that ladder and pretend I'm artistic. I add a line that might be the bridge of my nose, a curve that could be my upper lip, a sweep that I mean to be Brooke's jawline, the cup of her ear. I stand back to assess my work. It doesn't even look like two girls' faces, just shapes. I eye the little moth at the bottom of the wall, waiting for its wings to flutter.

I spend the next day as tiny-boned Heath Mineo. His gossip is of a different sort entirely. Kids sidle up to him, twenties soft in their palms, and murmur drug orders—a series of names and numbers I don't try to decode. I throw in a skeptical comment about Paige Wheeler's suicide when I can, but the burners are much too eager to believe it was suicide; they don't even listen.

I decide that I'm not too keen on being the school drug dealer. Not after what happened to Brooke. I wait until the guidance office is empty and squeeze the ill-gotten twenties into Mrs. Morello's canister for harelipped children. I've prepared for some resistance from Heath, a hearty shove for giving all his money away, and I'm surprised when there's nothing, not a stir. Maybe Heath has some ambivalence about his dealing, after all.

While I'm in the office, I retrieve Heath's locker combination from the school secretary, who seems unfazed that Heath would have forgotten it. I've resolved to find Heath's stash and flush it, and who cares how he explains that to himself tomorrow? But when I open his locker to look, a note falls at my feet. I stare at the folded square of paper resting on the toe of Heath's sneaker, then snatch it up and open it with a shiver of premonition.

It has ♀ with a five written under it.

I know that code. I know that blocky handwriting. In fact, I've received the same note myself.

So instead of joining the flow of students returning to class, I walk in the opposite direction, toward the forbidden bathroom, where I expect to find Lucas Hayes waiting for me.

Too bad I get stopped on the way by Principal Bosworth, who, it turns out, knows that Heath has Algebra II this period, located nowhere near the gym. He walks me all the way back to class, where Mrs. Kearny ignores me huffily, like I've personally wronged her and will now be punished with the silent treatment. It takes half the hour and repeated pleas before she hands over the hall pass.

"Two minutes," she says.

"Two," I agree, wrenching the pass from her pincer fingers.

I run all the way to the other end of the school in a minute flat, and as I run, I think about the note tucked in Heath's pocket. I think about how everyone else saw Lucas as this perfect specimen: gleaming smile, transcript, and trophies in the case. And I'd seen him that way, too, emphasis on the surface sparkle. Until I'd started to see him as someone else, someone who'd fix my physics project for me, someone nice, someone I might be able to like. But we'd been wrong about Lucas, my classmates and I. Or at least we'd been working with incomplete information. Turns out, Lucas is also the type of guy who has secret meetings with the school drug dealer. Turns out he's the type of guy who'll pretend he didn't know you, even after you're dead.

I round the corner and see the bathroom door in front of me. I push through it at a jog and am three steps in before I realize that my steps are splashing. I look down at my feet.

Water.

I hadn't noticed it at first, the *shhh!* of the faucets running. When I turn the corner, there's Lucas, standing in front of the overflowing sinks like he's guarding them from potential harm. The sinks wobble with the shine of water that pours over their sides. This is no simple paper-towel-stuffed drain; this is a full-on flooding.

"Did you do this?" I ask Lucas.

His smile is like a fishhook, and his voice has a sharp, sarcastic edge to it. "Nah, I just *happened* to walk in on it."

"Really?"

"Of course."

"We should go," I say. "The water's almost out the door."

Lucas tilts his head, his hair falling over one eye. "No. Let's stay."

"But they'll think we did it." I pause. "They'll think *I* did it."

"That's probably true," Lucas admits, shaking his head. "Karma, man. Sucks when it finally comes around again."

"What are you talking about? Why are you acting like this?"

"Like what?" he says.

"Are you *on* something?"

He laughs at this, a dry, narrow laugh. "Just high on life."

"I'm going," I tell him. "And I think you should, too."

"Really, Heath? Is that what *you* think I should do?"

"Yeah, it is," I say. "But stay if you want. I'm going."

I'm good as my word. I turn and splash back out of the bathroom and straight into Mrs. Morello and Principal Bosworth.

Three days' suspension for Lucas and Heath, and no one will listen when I protest that I, Heath, wasn't part of the flooding. As I've predicted, Mr. Bosworth fingers me as the ringleader. In fact, he keeps saying to Lucas, "You can tell us if you weren't a part of this, son." Lucas doesn't deny his guilt, but he doesn't exonerate Heath either. Guess Heath is the same as me, some guy Lucas doesn't know.

We sit in the office for two full periods waiting for the adults to fill out the requisite paperwork and make the parent-or-guardian phone calls. Our classmates peer through the glass walls as they pass, double-taking at the sight of Lucas and me awaiting punishment together. And so the rumors will be shifting again. Heath practically lives in the office, but I wonder what they'll say about Lucas, the school Boy Scout, the school hero, hauled in for the same crime. Mrs. Morello makes an impassioned plea for Mr. Bosworth to consider *where* the vandalism took place, that Lucas might be grappling with some very understandable issues around Brooke Lee's death.

"Yeah, right," Lucas says, only loud enough for me to hear it.

It's not until Heath's stepfather drives him away—as he turns out of the parking lot, I'm yanked from the backseat of the car and deposited on the school roof—that I remember Usha and the mural. The bell for sixth rang nearly half an hour ago. By the time I reach the hallway by the student parking lot, it's too late. Usha is standing on a ladder, drop cloth pooling on the floor below her. Any questions I might have had about what she would do with the mural are answered. She brandishes a paintbrush, dripping white, and swipes over the lines of Brooke's and my faces, turning them back into blank wall.

"No," I whisper.

It's gone, my connection to people, to life. She's erasing it, sweep by sweep. Erasing me. I stand there staring.

Maybe we should be trying to forget.

Until I feel someone staring just as intently at me.

Both Usha and I turn at the clang.

Greenvale Greene has dropped a can of paint. She kneels to pick it up, but she keeps glancing at me, her eyes wild under the brush of her bangs.

"What happened?" Usha says, and when Greenvale doesn't answer, she begins to climb down the ladder. "You okay?"

I step toward Greenvale. "Can you see me?"

She turns back to the paint, but a small moan escapes her mouth.

"Greenvale?" Usha says.

"You can," I say. "You can see me!"

I take another step.

Greenvale bolts.

14: GREENVALE

I FIND HER IN BROOKE'S BATHROOM, CURLED UP IN THE handicapped stall. It takes a good ten minutes of cajoling to get her to unlatch the door. When it swings open, she stares at me for a moment and then slides down the wall again, clasping her hands around her legs, tucking her knees to her chin. The floor is still damp from Lucas's flooding, but Greenvale doesn't seem to care.

"Hi," I say.

She expels a meek "Hey."

"You can see me, can't you?"

Just when I think she's not going to respond, she nods. "I can see all of you. You and Brooke Lee and that boy who sits in the art room."

"She can see us?" a voice says from over by the sinks.

At the sound of it, Greenvale slides to the back of the stall. I turn to find Brooke crouching on her death spot, peering curiously at Greenvale and me. She hadn't been there when I came in; she must have just crossed over the school property line.

"It's okay," I tell Greenvale. "It's just Brooke."

I beckon to Brooke, who peers around the edge of the stall door. "Brooke, Greenvale. Greenvale, Brooke."

"You can really see us?" Brooke asks.

Greenvale opens her mouth and closes it again.

"It's okay," I repeat. "She won't hurt you."

"Yeah," Brooke agrees amiably. "I can't even touch you. I'm a ghost. See?" She passes her hand through the metal door, which is probably less comforting than she intends it to be.

Greenvale emits a shaky laugh.

"How can you see us?" I ask.

"No one else can," Brooke adds.

"I-I don't know," Greenvale stutters. "I just can. You're just there."

"Could you always?" I ask.

"Not always."

"How long?"

"Three years ago, my grandpa had a stroke," she begins, then stops for a nervous swallow. "He moved in with us so my mom could take care of him."

"What does your grandpa have to do with—"

"Hush," I tell Brooke.

"He died in his sleep, in our house," she continues. "Mom sent me down to the basement to get the extra table leaf for the memorial service." She looks down at her fidgeting hands; they still under her gaze. "He was there, my grandpa, standing right there in the middle of the basement. I ran away that time, too. Upstairs. I locked myself in my room, but it wasn't good enough. I couldn't sleep or eat or . . . I kept thinking he was going to float up through the vents."

"That's why they sent you to Greenvale?"

"Greenvale Greene," she says. I wince, but she shrugs at the nickname. "I'm used to it."

97

"What did the doctors say?" Brooke asks.

"Nothing. I didn't tell them that I'd seen my dead grandpa, didn't tell my parents either. I'm not stupid. I knew what they'd think about that: crazy girl. I mean, cra*zier* girl. My parents didn't send me to Greenvale because I saw ghosts. They sent me because I wouldn't leave my room. The doctors diagnosed me with social anxiety. They said it happens in Japan sometimes, teenagers who won't leave their bedrooms. Maybe there are ghosts in Japan, too. Anyway, they let me out after a couple weeks."

"And when you got back home?" I ask. "Was your grandpa still there? In the basement?"

"He's gone." She looks down. "He never came back. I should've talked to him. I should've said good-bye."

"I'm sorry," I say.

"Do you know where he went?" Brooke asks.

"He was just gone. He's not in the basement anymore. Not in the house. Or if he is, I can't see him." She shakes her head, then looks up at me through her bangs; her eyes underneath are a light greenish gray. And pretty, I realize.

"So you just watched us?" Brooke asks. "This whole time you've been watching us?"

"Not watching. Just . . . I'd see you. The first time I saw you, I ran away. All the way home." She dips her head bashfully. "It was a few weeks after your . . . your death. You were walking down the hall after"—she turns to me—"Paige, actually."

"Stalker," I tease, but Brooke's attention is fixed on Greenvale.

"Can other people see us?" she asks.

"I don't know. I don't think so. I think it's just me."

"I know you were helping Usha with the—" I start to say, but Greenvale interrupts me with a squeak.

"Oh, no. Usha!" She puts her hands to her face. "I dropped her paint. I ran away. She'll think I'm crazy." She sighs. "Like the rest of them."

"Maybe not," I say. "You could tell her about me. You could explain how—" But I stop at the stricken look on her face. "No, I know. Of course you can't."

"I'm sorry," she says. "But I can't. They'll send me back."

"It's okay. I understand."

"And I'm sorry I ran away from you."

"You were scared."

"And I'm also sorry . . ." She hides behind her bangs again.

"What?" Brooke says.

She whispers, "I'm sorry you're dead."

"Thank you," I say, then add, "Thank you, Harriet."

15: SPREADING RUMORS

EVEN THOUGH HARRIET CAN SEE ME, I FEEL MORE INVISIBLE than ever. Usha has painted over the mural, and I still haven't been able to undo the rumor of my supposed suicide. The next morning dawns, and the only not-so-terrible news is that Mr. Fisk has left the drop cloth up to let all that white paint dry. I don't have much time left until the mural is really and truly gone, only a day or two more when people will pass that drop cloth and think of me. There's no more time for half measures.

I decide to inhabit Chris Rackham, the roundest of the well-rounders, class president and likely valedictorian. In class, I try to keep a straight face as everyone, including the teachers, turns to me for the answers. When I was alive, I rarely participated in class discussions. It seemed like such an act, so obvious what the teachers were waiting to hear, so easy to say the words to please them. But, hey, I'm a well-rounder now. I've always had the answers; now I may as well give them. And everyone is glad that things have gone as expected.

Funny that I am not *un*glad about this. Class, it turns out, goes by more quickly when you're part of the conversation. I decide that maybe the well-rounders aren't completely dumb about acting smart. I discover something else, too. If I answer the teacher's questions, I can sometimes sneak in a question or two of my own.

"I read that Andy Warhol was gay," I say when Mr. Fisk calls on me (for the fifth time that hour) in art class. "Was he?" This question is for Evan, but I don't dare glance at him sitting invisibly on the cupboard behind me.

My comment earns a few titters and a shout of "Awesome!"

"Yes," Mr. Fisk agrees gamely, "and in Warhol's time, there were actually laws that made it illegal to . . ." And on he goes.

After the bell has rung, I approach Mr. Fisk's desk, where he stirs a soup of papers between his long fingers.

"Thanks for telling us about Andy Warhol," I say.

"Certainly." Mr. Fisk looks up. "Thanks for asking."

"I just thought it could be helpful for some people who might be thinking about their, you know, orientation."

"I agree." Mr. Fisk leaves the papers altogether. His eyebrows draw together. Serious teacher face. I know where this is headed. "Is that something you're worried about, Chris?"

"No, not me. At least, I don't think so," I add because I don't know the inner halls of Chris Rackham's heart or even the topiary lining its front walk.

"It's all right not to be sure," Mr. Fisk says.

"Yeah, I know. But, really, it's a friend who's wondering."

"Ah," Mr. Fisk says. "A friend."

"Not a 'friend' that's me. A real friend. He exists."

Mr. Fisk smiles. "I wasn't trying to imply it was you. It's just I had a friend like that, too." The angles of his smile have shifted somehow into something sad. *Your mouth really should be bent the opposite way,* I want to tell him. "Are you worried about your friend?" he asks.

"I just want him to . . . be okay with himself."

Mr. Fisk closes his eyes, right there in the classroom. "I want that for every student." He opens them. "Maybe you could invite him to a GSA meeting. Gay-Straight Alliance. Every other Wednesday after school."

"I don't know if he'd go to that."

"Maybe if you came with him."

"Yeah, maybe. Thanks."

I turn, eager to see Evan's reaction to this. But the back cupboard holds only art supplies, not, as I'd hoped, an attentive ghost. All that awkward teacher conversation, and Evan hasn't even bothered to listen to it.

And now for lunch, and the real reason I've chosen to inhabit Chris Rackham. Not only was Chris elected class president by the sheer tens of students who had bothered to fill out a ballot, but his mom is superintendent of our school district. There is no one more trustworthy at Paul Revere High. People will have to believe him when he says I fell.

I time it for midway through lunch, the well-rounders reaching the pudding cups at the bottoms of their brown bags. There's a lull in the conversation as butterscotch is wordlessly traded for vanilla and foils are peeled back with a snick of plastic. I wait for the silence to peak. At just the right moment, Kelsey Pope obliges me by standing up on her chair and waving one of the ponies over to her with a giddy yell.

"Someone sure needs a lot of attention," I make Chris say, looking meaningfully at Kelsey.

"She's a pleasure-seeking monster," Whitney Puryear agrees grimly. "We used to be best friends for, like, all of middle school. Did you know that?"

"No," I say honestly.

"Well, we were. She used to say," Whitney sits up extra straight, widens her eyes, and heaves an imaginary sheath of hair over her shoulder, "'Whitney, do you ever feel like you'll love everyone, and no one will ever love you back?'"

"Awww!" the well-rounders chorus faux pity in a minor key.

"That must have been before she got breasts," I quip, and the rounders all look at me, stunned.

"Chris, ouch!" Whitney says.

"Yes, people, you heard it here. Chris just said *that*," another one says.

"Just kidding," I mumble, reminding myself to act more like Chris, less like me.

"Well, everyone frigging loves her now anyway." Whitney rolls her eyes.

"Do they?" I ask. "I heard she made up this nasty rumor about—"

"Paige Wheeler?" one of the rounders cuts in. "Yeah, a kid in calc was saying that maybe Kelsey made that up."

"Right. Exactly. Did anyone else hear that?" I ask, thinking of my hours of careful rumor spreading. I am awarded with noncommittal noises.

"If you ask me, that girl totally jumped," Whitney says.

"Totally," one of the others agrees. "Nancy Kim was there on the roof. She said you couldn't fall off. There's a ledge thing—you can see it from the ground. You'd have to step up onto it."

"But what if Paige stepped up onto the ledge and then slipped?" I counter.

"Why would she step up onto the ledge?" someone asks.

"Because . . . I don't know. To see a little farther, to be a little higher. To be daring."

They look at me blankly.

"Yeah," Whitney says. "She totally jumped."

"But she didn't," I say. "Kelsey made it up."

"How would you know that?" Whitney asks.

I can hardly say, *Because I'm Paige and I didn't jump.* "Because of my mom," I say instead.

All the well-rounders look up from their puddings now. "Your mom told you something about the suicide?" one of them asks.

"She did." I lean in. "But she made me promise not to tell anyone."

"Maybe you shouldn't," half the table replies, while the other half urges, "Tell *us.*" Thus follows a debate about the ethics and loopholes of parental secrets. The matter is finally decided by Whitney Puryear's unimpeachable argument: "Well, you have to tell us now."

"All right." I lower my voice. "But you have to promise not to say anything."

They all promise.

In my hushed tone, I say, "Kelsey Pope is being investigated for slander."

"By the police?" a girl asks skeptically.

"Of course not," I say. "By the school board."

"Really?" Whitney says. "Kelsey's under investigation?" She looks pleased.

"Yeah." I gird myself against the deep unconscious part of Chris that will push against this bald lie. The push comes, and I hold on until it passes. "The forensic examiners looked at the trajectory of the fall and the angle of the body." (I silently thank my own mother's addiction to trashy crime shows.) "It was definitely a fall. An accident."

"They can tell that?"

"Of course. It's science."

"It *is* science," someone else adds. "It's not like how they show it on those TV shows—twenty minutes with a microscope, and you find the magic hair. In reality, it's legitimate."

"Exactly." I nod. "Science."

"Then the suicide was just a rumor? That's the slander?"

"Yep."

"So Kelsey lied."

"Yep," I say again.

"What's going to happen to her?" Whitney asks.

"I don't know. Maybe nothing. They're just looking into it. Besides, it's just a rumor."

"Yeah, but that's a pretty sick rumor," Whitney says. "I mean, think about how Paige Wheeler's friends must feel. Or her parents."

"Right," I say. "Exactly."

"If it were up to me, I'd suspend her," Whitney continues. "Or expel her. Something permanent-record for sure."

The others voice their agreement in unison.

I hide a smile. "You guys won't tell anyone, right?"

The next morning, I stand under the drop cloth and wait anxiously to see how Chris's new rumor is faring. I hear nothing from the early arrivals, and my mood starts to sink under the weight of another failed plan. The thick of students marches in minutes before the bell, and still nothing. It's nowhere.

I was so sure it was going to work. Everyone knows Chris Rackham wouldn't lie; he is always completely and totally honest. And besides, yesterday at lunch, the well-rounders had all seemed to believe him.

"What's wrong with you?" I grumble at the milling crowd.

They walk on, oblivious. *People want to believe bad things*, I tell myself, glaring around at my classmates. *They want to believe the most shocking story. They see you as the worst version of yourself.*

Then, at the end of the hall, I hear my name. It's Whitney Puryear, her voice loud enough for everyone to hear. Chris Rackham stands in front of her, tugging nervously at his hair, then his jacket collar.

"So you made it up?" she says. "The whole thing?"

I try to rush over to them, to inhabit Chris before he can answer, but there are too many people between us, many of them stopped and gawking at Whitney and Chris, many of them thinking my name. If I run through them, I may well inhabit someone other than Chris. I try to weave through the gaps between people, but I already know I can't get there in time.

Chris says something hushed, and Whitney responds with, "But there's no investigation?"

And I'm close enough now to hear Chris say, "No investigation, no anything. My mom didn't say anything to me about Kelsey Pope or Paige Wheeler."

Whitney wrinkles her nose and booms, "Why would you tell us all that, then?"

I've reached them now, and they're both thinking about me, but instead of inhabiting them, I hang back, curious to know what Chris will say next.

"I think . . ." He takes a breath and lets it out, whistling through his nose. "I just wanted to see if you'd believe me. I don't know. I got an impulse and then I was saying it. I'm sorry. I don't know why I did it. As soon as I said it, I felt terrible."

"Have you told the others?"

"Yesterday, as soon as I could. But I couldn't find you."

"My mom picked me up early. I had a dentist's appointment," Whitney says, sounding more put out about being the last one to know the truth than about being lied to in the first place.

"You didn't tell anyone, did you?" Chris asks. "About what I said?"

"Maybe just a couple people," she answers slowly.

"Well, take it back," Chris says evenly. "Tell them the truth."

"What am I even supposed to say?"

Chris shrugs. "Tell them I'm a liar."

No, I think as the bell rings and Chris and Whitney disappear along with my brilliant plan. *Kelsey is the liar.*

And you, something in me whispers. *You lied, too.*

"Paige," a voice says at my back. I turn to find Evan's pale eyes and each one of his many freckles blaring concern.

"Why aren't you in class?" I point up. "That was the late bell."

"I was going and then I saw you standing here."

"I was just . . ." I turn around in a slow circle in the middle of the empty hallway and stop back where I started. "I give up."

"You give up?"

"I give up. I accept it. Everyone thinks I'm a jumper, a suicide."

"People are going to think what they think," Evan says. "But you know the truth. You know who you are."

"Do I?" I ask. "I don't know."

"Well, then"—he nods curtly—"*I* know who you are."

I can't take his pitying expression anymore. I stick out my tongue.

"Yeah," he says. "See? That about sums you up."

16: THE NOMINEES

FISK MUST HAVE FORGOTTEN ABOUT THE DROP CLOTH
entirely because it's still tacked on the wall the next day. It's not as
effective as it was at first, though. Fewer and fewer people look at it
when they pass by; fewer still think of me. One of the only people
who does spare me a thought is Kelsey Pope. She canters in with
her herd of ponies, glancing at it once, then twice, each time her
thoughts calling my name.

I haven't wanted to inhabit Kelsey, haven't wanted to be trapped
in her perfect form. I'd told myself it was a last resort. If all other
attempts to kill the suicide rumor failed, then I would make Kelsey
tell everyone how she'd made it up. But after what happened with
Chris Rackham, I've learned that even that won't work. As soon as
I'm no longer controlling Kelsey, she'll just take back anything I've
said. She'll just lie again.

I give up.

Kelsey looks back at the drop cloth a third time, thinking my
name. I trail after the ponies, both bothered and intrigued that

Kelsey is thinking so much about me. Is she regretting the rumor she started? Or, more likely, is she planning to say something else next?

When they reach Kelsey's locker, the group of ponies around it is somehow larger than ever.

And it's jumping up and down.

"Kelsey!" they shriek. And somehow they reform their circle with Kelsey and me at its center.

"You're a nominee!" they say as they jump, their voices rising and falling with gravity. "For prom!"

"Congratulations!" they all gush, as if Kelsey has already won. As if she isn't nominated queen for every dance. As if a paste-crown coronation in the school gym is anything but absurd. This time when Kelsey thinks of me, I *don't* hesitate. I step forward. Suddenly, I'm balancing on tippy-heeled boots and counterbalancing a dozen pounds of hair. Worse, there's what feels like a pebble stuck inside my mouth. I poke my tongue at it and find the back to Kelsey's piercing. The ponies press in around me, expressions morphing from gleeful to vaguely confused.

"You're not smiling," one of them notices.

"You're not jumping," one says.

"She's always nominated," another adds archly. "Maybe it's not a big deal."

"You know who *wasn't* nominated this time?" the first pony says in my ear, and before I can voice a guess, "Lucas Hayes. He's gotten *so* weird."

"Good move dumping him."

"Kelsey always knows which way the wind is blowing," someone whispers with acid, but when I turn to see who has said this, a camera phone is in my face, and two other ponies have appeared giddily at my side. "Here they are," the pony photographer announces, then lowers the camera. "Kelsey, you're *still* not smiling. Let's try again: Here they are, the prom court!"

"Well, except for Usha Das," another adds.

"Wait," I say, "Usha was nominated?"

"Yeah, she's the fourth nominee."

"Wow," I breathe, smiling. Yes, the whole thing is still absurd, but if someone is going to be prom queen, it *should* be Usha.

"Yeah, wow," one of the ponies says to me. "My reaction exactly."

"Of course, you know why," another adds.

"Why?" I ask.

"Because of *you know*."

"She means pity," the first one says smoothly.

"Pity?" I say.

"People feel sorry for her because her friend killed herself."

I cock my head. "And what about us? Why are we nominated?"

The other nominees look at each other.

"Because people like us," one of them says slowly.

"Do they really?" I ask. "I don't think they do."

"What's gotten into you?" the other one says, nostrils flaring.

I shrug. "Call it honesty."

The ponies look like they have a decisively different name for it. I smile innocently at them. Kelsey is nominated for prom queen? Fine. Let's see if she wins.

"What happened to your regular clothes?" one of the bolder ponies asks as I join them in the cafeteria line an hour later.

The others outright stare at the wrinkled T-shirt and sweat-pants I pulled out of the lost-and-found bin in the locker room. Kelsey had stormed and bucked inside me, but I forced her feet through the elastic cuffs of the sweatpants, her head through the dank cotton of the shirt. I'd gotten the idea for the clothes from Greenvale, though I'd refrained from throwing Kelsey's original outfit in the toilet. Just.

Anger runs through me and, with it, a sense of rightness and power. I've been thinking about it all morning. I know that I can't make Kelsey say anything she wouldn't say herself, or she'll just take it back as soon as she's herself again. But I can make Kelsey *do* things, things that she can't undo later. Kelsey ruined my reputation? Well, I can ruin hers right back.

The sweatpants Kelsey now wears are a stained (with what? don't ask) baby blue, elastic at the ankles. The shirt advocates for some team called the Fighting Pelicans, though it's not clear what type of sports team the Fighting Pelicans are or even that the large-beaked bird is a pelican. He looks more like a vulture with a top hat. Kelsey's hair? In pigtails. High ones. Kelsey had resisted me again and again, especially when I yanked on the sweatpants, but I've gotten good at planting my feet on the ground of my own will. It's like standing still in the middle of the hall just as the warning bell rings. Shoulders bump you on every side; some people will even run smack into you, but you have to stay standing.

"What? You don't like it?" I try not to show my amusement as the ponies struggle to find the right answer for this question. *Come on, you can say it,* I think. *It's hideous.* Even strangers are turning to look.

"Is it a Spirit Day?" a pony asks hopefully.

"Nope. I just thought I'd try something different."

"It's different, all right," one whispers to another.

"Actually," one of them says, "my sister's friends at Bard dress like that."

"They do?" I ask. "Really?"

"I've seen it. It's, like, the kind of style where you don't try too hard."

"Besides, you'd look good in anything, Kelsey."

They all nod in agreement. Ponies. The worst part is that they're right. Kelsey looks okay—maybe better than okay, maybe hip, daring, cute, even—in wrinkled lost-and-found gym clothes.

"The line's moving," I say, and sigh.

I let the ponies go ahead of me, gathering their salads and soft pretzels. When I get to the counter, I slap down dessert after dessert—slabs of brownie with cracked sugar tops, squares of cake thick with frosting, two wavering towers of soft-serve ice cream—until my tray is laden with small circular plates. Kelsey rages around inside me, and for a moment, I lose my grip on the tray and drop it with a splat. Everyone around me claps sarcastically. The lunch ladies sigh as I reload a fresh tray, but they don't make me pay twice.

When I slide my tray onto our table, the ponies stare at it.

"Hungry?" one of them ventures.

They share looks.

"That's brave," another notes.

"You trying for bulimia? Induce the urge to vomit?"

"What do you mean?" I take up a forkful. "Looks good to me."

They watch me eat the tray's contents with big eyes and repulsed mouths. But when I take the last bite of the last piece of cake, they start applauding, this time in earnest.

No luck with rudeness. No luck with clothing. No luck with food. On the way to art class, I'm racking my brains for what reputation-killing move to try next when I literally run into my pony escort, which has halted in the art room doorway.

"Oh, God, look," one of them whispers.

I peer over their shoulders and see Wes Nolan sitting at his table, sketching. "So what?" I say.

"So his nose is practically touching the page."

"Page. Paige!" the other one squeals, hitting her friend. "Funny!"

Both Usha and Harriet look over from where they stand at Mr. Fisk's desk. "Shhhh!" the other pony says, managing to be even louder. "Do you think he *you knows* to it?"

"Ew! Gross!" They begin jostling each other over the grossness of this.

I look from one pony to the other. "I'm going to ask Wes Nolan to prom," I announce. I wait for resistance from Kelsey, but this time, there's nothing.

The ponies, however, react. "You're *what?*"

"Asking Wes to prom."

"Right?" one says, eyes glittering. "He can give you a corsage of weeds from his backyard!"

"And you can spend the dance outside watching him smoke pot!" adds the other.

"But"—the first one makes a mock-sad face—"you'll probably never live up to the memory of Paige Wheeler."

"No, seriously. I'm asking him." I slide between them and up to Wes's table, which yes, carries the slight scent of smoke. Wes looks up at the sound of my approach. I wait for him to grin and say something smart-ass, as usual, but he offers only a blank stare.

"Hey," I say.

"Hey." Still no grin, and I wonder what is wrong with him.

Now that I'm here standing in front of him, my heart is clomping as loud as Kelsey's stupid boots, even though it's not me standing here. It's Kelsey and Wes Nolan. Who cares?

The thing is, I've never asked a boy to a dance.

Or anywhere.

"Wes?"

"Yeah?"

I take a breath and say, loud enough to carry, "Would you like to go to prom with me?"

By the end of my question, the already quiet room holds not even a pencil scratch. I glance over my shoulder. Everyone is staring, including Mr. Fisk, who doesn't even bother to tell me to get back to my seat. The ponies are gawping. Wes mumbles something.

"Prom is kind of stupid, I know. And we don't have to do the corsage thing," I barrel on. "Or the dinner."

"I said no," he repeats quietly, and I vaguely realize that he already said this a second ago, but I talked right over him.

It seems like I'm standing there forever. "But I'm Kelsey Pope."

He nods. "You are."

"But, but . . . ," I stammer, "I'm not joking. Did you think I was joking?"

"Why would you be joking?"

I put a hand to my face. My skin is hot. I can't turn around and face all of those people staring at me, though a blush on Kelsey probably looks rosy and inviting, unlike the splotchy skin disease of my blushes.

But that's just it, isn't it? It's not me who Wes said *no* to. It's Kelsey. And, wasn't this what I wanted? To embarrass Kelsey Pope? To ruin her? And then I realize, Wes saying *no* is way better than if he'd said *yes*.

"Guess it was a long shot." I smile. "Let me know if you change your mind. I'll still be available."

"Um, sure." Wes's blank expression clouds with puzzlement. He drops his eyes to his sketchbook, leaving me to walk the entire length of the room back to the ponies.

"What was that?" one of them asks. "Some kind of joke?"

"Not at all."

"Yeah, right." She nudges the other. "Who would want to go to prom with Wes Nolan?"

"I don't know," I say. "Maybe I would."

The ponies become suddenly and intently focused on their art projects. They're the only ones, though. The rest of the class bubbles with whispers and glances. I smile around the room, pleased that finally there's no one, not even Greenvale Greene, willing to meet my eyes and smile back.

17: THE OUTCAST

WES WAS THE TIPPING POINT. BY THE LAWS OF RIDICULOUS HIGH school logic, making up lies about a dead girl doesn't touch Kelsey's reputation, but getting rejected by Wes Nolan makes her the joke of the school. The next week, Brooke, Evan, and I follow behind Kelsey. Even the dead kids are interested in the fallout from Kelsey's botched prom proposal. Me especially. And this time, I'm not disappointed. Kelsey walks to her locker in a rush of whispers, everyone repeating the same rumor that they've all already heard: *Wes Nolan turned her down. Her! Kelsey Pope!* Their whispers lilt with excitement, and their eyes shine with glee. I realize that they've been hoping for this. They're glad to see her brought low. And I wonder if this is what popularity really is, people waiting to hate you in the open.

The burners are the worst. Or at least the loudest. We pass a cluster of them by the drinking fountain.

"Hey, Pope! Don't you have something to ask me?" they call.

"No, me!"

"Me!" the girls chime in. "Me!"

"I'll even buy you that corsage," Heath Mineo, fresh from his suspension, adds, somehow managing to make the word *corsage* sound lewd.

For once, Wes Nolan doesn't seem to find the joke funny. He ducks his head and disappears down the hall in the opposite direction, which only makes his friends laugh harder.

"This is too much," Evan says.

"Not even close," Brooke tells him. "People should get what they deserve."

"What did she do to deserve this? Ask the wrong person to prom?"

"No," Brooke says. "She spread rumors about Paige's death. It's karma, bitch. Right, Paige?"

Both of them look at me.

"I'm not going to feel bad for Kelsey Pope. Why should I?"

"Because you know what it feels like to have a rumor spread about you," Evan replies.

"Yes," I say. "Exactly."

It doesn't take long for Evan and Brooke to grow bored with Kelsey's long walks down barbed hallways. I keep following her anyway, until a near-silent lunch with the ponies and another razzing by two burner girls sends her to the office with complaints of an oncoming migraine. Maybe the gossip has reached even the teachers, because they let her sign out without protest. I follow her all the way to the school doors and watch her cross the parking lot, hair whipping in the wind, chin tucked down into her coat.

She lied about you, I tell myself. *She deserves what she gets.*

I'm sitting up on the roof when the final bell rings and, a moment later, dozens of voices begin to float up to me like balloons. Another day of school done. I peer down at them, the tiny people trickling out in pairs or clusters. I stand and stretch, thinking that I might sit in on the German Club meeting, which almost sounds like English if you listen to it sideways. I'm halfway across the roof when the tiny floating voices turn from balloons to firecrackers, screeching up into the air.

The sound is so terrible, so startling, that I nearly lose my hover.

They're screaming. Everyone is screaming.

Then, pitched up over the screams, a squeal of breaks.

A suck of breath.

A crash.

I run back to the edge of the roof, scrambling up onto my death spot and looking down below.

There they are:

One set of tire tracks curls, the arc and color of shrieking rubber.

Two bodies.

One on the hood of the car.

Another sprawled on the ground in front of it.

By the time I reach the parking lot, there's already a circle of people around the crash site. A few are on their cells. I hear the words "fast" and "nowhere" and a girl crying so gently it sounds like she's singing a wordless song. Others have their phones held high, videotaping, their arms slowly waving with the weight of them, and I think of a concert when the audience holds up their lighters aflame. Most of the onlookers, though, stand in a stunned silence.

The crowd is thick, but I find pockets of emptiness. I duck through here and there, finally walking out into the space at the crowd's center.

I recognize him at a distance by his shoe, which sits, empty of foot, in front of me. A week ago, I was wearing that sneaker. The note from Lucas had dropped out onto its toe. I look across the blacktop. Heath Mineo lies facedown on the ground, knees tucked to his chest and arms thrown wide, a white sock peeking out from beneath his crumpled body.

Two burners stand over him.

"I think I see breathing," one of them says, his voice loud with shock.

"Don't move him," the other warns, adding, "right?" He looks blindly at the crowd around him. "Right?"

No one answers.

There was a second body, I think fuzzily. On the car.

I circle the car, with each step, a new sliver of the body on its hood becoming visible: a shirtsleeve, a skinny arm, a strand of lank hair. One more step, and I hear myself gasp.

She lies curled over the dashboard, still half in the driver's seat, her upper body resting on the hood. At first, I think she's crying, but then I realize those are tears of safety glass in the corners of her closed eyes.

It's Harriet Greene.

18: AFTER THE ACCIDENT

"I DIDN'T SEE *HER*, JUST THE CAR," CHRIS RACKHAM TELLS THE police. "It came around the end of the row there."

"I heard it before I saw it," biblical Erin says. "It made that sound, you know, that screaming-car sound. The tires."

"At first it seemed like someone messing around, trying to get attention." Lane Cosgrove shakes her ponytail. "But then we all realized . . . This. Isn't. A. Joke."

"We jumped out of the way," one of the burners says, and the officer writes a few quick lines. "Heath was just next to us. He jumped away, too. But then the car . . . it turned, like *at* Heath."

"It veered to the left there, where it hit him." Whitney Puryear points to the tire tracks curling between the two rows of cars. "The brakes squealed anyway. But it was too late. You could see it was going to hit him."

"She broke through the windshield," Joe Schultz says. "There was glass."

"She didn't know him." The burner shakes his head. "I don't think so, anyway. I don't think she really knew anyone."

"Maybe she had some sort of . . ." Lane pauses to pick the word carefully. "*episode*. Did any of the others tell you? Sophomore year, she was in a place, you know . . . a *facility*."

They call off classes for the next three days. The adults still come in, though, and hold an amazing number of meetings. Evan, Brooke, and I haunt the main office, waiting for news about Harriet and Heath, which arrives the next afternoon. Heath is conscious, but with a concussion and a broken collarbone, leg, and three ribs. He'll finish the year out in the hospital and then at home.

Harriet has yet to wake up. They're officially calling it a coma.

Over the following days, the silent crowd around the crash site fractures into a chaos of delayed reactions. The buttons on the secretary's phone blink their demon eyes, and her litany of "hold-pleaseholdpleaseholdplease" begins to loop in my head. Mrs. Morello and Mr. Bosworth hold near-hourly meetings, outlining the new parking lot regulations, the added trauma counseling, and screening for "at-risk" students.

The teachers come out of these meetings shaking their heads.

"What a year!" one of them groans.

"This place is cursed," another says.

When I'm not following the drama in the office, I sit up on my death spot and look out over the parking lot, knowing that in the hospital across town, Harriet lies on a tide deeper than sleep, shallower than death. I remember her small, phlegmy voice whispering, *I'm sorry that you're dead.*

It all starts to seem petty, the rumors, my reputation, my revenge. What does it matter compared to Mr. and Mrs. Greene sitting stiffly in Bosworth's office, a crumpled Kleenex twitching in Mrs. Greene's hand? What does it matter compared to Harriet on the hood of the car, safety glass tears in the corners of her eyes? If she dies, I wonder, will she awake in the hospital? Or will she appear down below, a pale blinking girl in the dark lake of the parking lot?

They bring the students back the following Monday. Most opt for the school bus, and the student parking lot is left two-thirds empty. My classmates are, days later, both sedated and enlivened by the car crash. They talk about it with the exhausted giddiness of kids who have stayed up too late at a slumber party. I wait by the mural sheet, which seems to have been permanently forgotten in the aftermath of Paul Revere High School's latest tragedy. Forgotten, too, is what the mural memorializes. No one looks at it anymore. No one thinks of me. So this is what it feels like to be forgotten.

Not forgotten is the shame of Kelsey Pope.

She arrives late, and I know that walk. She's spent the entire morning, while getting ready for school, telling herself to be tough. She'll show them she doesn't care, even though they still titter and whisper. Which they still do. I follow after, wondering how long she'll be able to keep it up.

Turns out, not long.

The hall is full when Kelsey reaches her locker. No ponies gather around it. No surprise. Kelsey doesn't glance over to where they are gathered at another pony's locker. She keeps her eyes on her own locker, spinning the dial and giving it a yank.

Hundreds of prom tickets spill out at her feet.

We, all of us in the hall, stare at the pastel slips of paper scattered around Kelsey like confetti. Kelsey stares, too, her eyes surprised at first, until she picks up one slip and then drops it fluttering to the floor.

Even from a few yards back, I can see that the ticket is professionally printed. *The well-rounders*, I think. They're the ones who organize the prom, who print the tickets. It takes less than a second for me to spot Whitney Puryear, her face lit with an anticipation almost like hunger.

The hallway explodes in sound. It's not laughter, not all of it, but enough of it is. I watch as Kelsey's eyes fill with tears.

This is it. Exactly what I'd engineered, exactly what I'd said I'd wanted. How is vindication supposed to feel? It should feel like the parts snap into place. It should feel like eating a bowl of warm, thick soup on a cold day. It should feel like suddenly you're solid again.

I watch the tears tremble in Kelsey's eyes and feel nothing.

Suddenly, I find myself stepping through people, directly through their mouths curled in laughter, their hands lifted to shield a whisper, their narrowed, judgmental eyes. I arrive in front of Kelsey.

"Think of me," I order. "You dumb pony, think of me."

But why would she?

Maybe because my old best friend steps out into the middle of the hall and shouts, "Shut up!" Usha balls her hands on her hips. "All of you, shut up!"

Kelsey stares at Usha, tears finally spilling over her cheeks, cutting across the expression of confusion on her face. She opens her mouth, but before she can speak, her voice thinks my name: *Paige*. It's enough.

I turn her around, chin lifted—damn the tears, damn the tickets, damn the laughter—and walk her through the crowd, a queen through the jackals, until the laughter fades away behind us.

And that's how it remains for the next week and a half. Every day, I wait until Kelsey thinks of me, then I inhabit her. I take her through her day—classes, lunch, worst are hallways—like the whispers and stares don't exist. She doesn't push back at me now, but then again, I don't do anything she wouldn't do herself.

Evan starts to ask where I've been. Even with Fisk's classes, he's started to notice that I'm not around.

"I'm here and there," I say lightly.

"You're where and where?" he asks.

I almost tell him. But I can't. It's the same feeling as when I couldn't tell Usha about my hook-ups with Lucas. I don't know how to explain why I've been doing what I've been doing. I just didn't think revenge would feel like this. Shameful. Petty. Mean. All the things I've accused Kelsey of, now it's me.

The next Wednesday, two weeks since the car accident, I walk Kelsey out of the cafeteria and see Wes and his burner friends clustered in the hall that leads to art class. Though Kelsey has to sit across the room from Wes in art, I've been trying to skirt him elsewhere because, maddeningly, no matter how I try to avoid it, my eyes always somehow land on his. As they do now. Before his friends even see me, Wes's eyes catch mine. Fortunately, there's a door a few steps away.

I duck into Brooke's bathroom to wait for the burners to disperse, but as I turn the corner to the sinks, I freeze.

Lucas stands in the same exact spot where he stood on the afternoon when he guarded the flooding sinks. I hadn't seen him since we'd sat together in Principal Bosworth's office, though I knew he must have been back from his suspension. It surprises me that I'd forgotten about him, the boy I used to look for at every ring of the bell. The girl with him is young, maybe only a freshman, though she's trying hard to look older, with a mouth dark as poisoned fruit and clunky boots that must make each step heavy. She floats up from the boots as if they're the only thing holding her to the ground, her head tilted back, her painted lips the highest point of her body. Lucas's mouth presses down on hers.

I step back into the shadow of the entranceway, watching them. The kiss stretches on for minutes that must in reality be only seconds, and I can do nothing but stare. It looks different from the way he'd kissed me, as if her lips actually are a fruit he's downing in bites, no regard for stem or seeds. It's the girl who finally pulls free; the lower half of Lucas's face is ripe with her dark lipstick.

"Do you want to know where it was?" Lucas asks.

She nods, her eyes wide.

Lucas points to the place on the floor by the sinks: Brooke's death spot. Then, he cocks his head and says, "You should lie down on it."

"Lie down?" she repeats uncertainly. "Like, on the floor?"

"Come on," Lucas says.

"I don't know."

"But if I wanted you to?"

With a smile that might be a grimace, she does. And when he bends down to kiss her there on the floor, I finally regain the ability to move.

Maybe we should be trying to forget.

Harriet's safety glass tears.

Kelsey's real tears.

The sketch of the girl under the tree.

She's just some girl who died.

It's too much.

I don't care about them.

Any of them.

I don't care.

I don't care.

These tears mean I don't care.

I run past Wes and the burner boys, their faces blurring through the scrim of my tears. I run past Usha, nearly knocking her from her ladder. The late bell rings, but I don't turn back. I slam the doors out to the parking lot and race across the soccer fields behind the school, their grass sucked gray and dry from the winter that just passed. I find a stretch of brick wall and slide to the ground. Here they are, tears I couldn't cry before, wet on my cheeks and hands.

"Hey," a voice says between half-caught breaths. "Hey, there."

I look up, and he's standing there, all shaggy hair and tattered coat. He wavers as the tears rise to my eyes, then clears as they fall.

"What are you doing here, Wes Nolan?"

"I followed you," he says, adding, "barely. You run fast."

"This isn't what it looks like," I tell him.

"What does it look like?"

"Like I'm upset."

He cocks his head. "You're not upset?"

"Don't look at me. I'm all tears and snot."

"Okay. I won't look." He turns away gamely. "So things have been pretty rough, huh?"

"No kidding," I say, then I realize what he must mean: that things have been rough for Kelsey because he turned her down. "I'm not upset over you, you know."

He raises his eyebrows, and I wonder if that sounded insulting. I wonder, after that, why I even care if it did.

"I saw Lucas Hayes in the bathroom," I explain. "He was making out with some burner."

"A burner?" Wes asks. "Like on a stove?"

"No. A burner like a girl who burns things—cigarettes, pot—who smokes things."

"Oh. Like me," he says.

"Yeah," I say uncomfortably. "I guess, yeah."

"A burner," he tries out the word, smiles at it. "I like that."

"It's supposed to be an insult."

"Okay." He smiles wider. "I still like it."

"Of course you do."

"You used to go out with Lucas Hayes, right?"

"Last year."

"So you still like him, huh?"

I bite Kelsey's lip and look across the field at the burners' circle where I used to wait, listening for the soft crush of pine needles that would mark Lucas's step, my heart beating at the possibility of that sound, my ears echoing with the absence of it, my mind protesting that I didn't care one way or the other. "Well, I did," I admit. "I liked him. I liked Lucas Hayes." And I laugh because I did. I really did like him. Prince Basketball. Mr. Gleam Tooth. High Testo himself. Lucas Hayes.

Wes nods. "Most girls seem to."

"Yeah. Most girls," I scoff. But in this case, most girls was me. "But I don't anymore." And as I say it, I know that it's true. I don't. I couldn't like someone who said that, who said I was some girl who died. "I think that maybe I liked the idea of him more than the actual him: Lucas Hayes."

"Lucas Hayes," Wes repeats.

"It's embarrassing, but . . ."

"If it's embarrassing, you have to tell."

"No, if it's embarrassing, I don't have to tell."

"Come on. You can make up for insulting me."

I smacked his arm. "You liked the insult."

"I like lots of things," he says.

"Fine. Here it is. It's embarrassing because I thought it made me special, because Lucas Hayes was special, and he'd chosen me. Turns out, I could have been anyone."

"You?" Wes says softly. "But you're Kelsey Pope, remember?"

I look up to see if he's mocking me, and he is, but in the nicest way possible.

"Can I tell you what really happened? In the bathroom?"

He nods.

I comb the grass next to me, all in one direction, then all in the other. "It wasn't that they were kissing." I shake my head, still not understanding what I'd seen, only understanding what it made me feel, sick and scared. "They were, then they stopped. And then he asked her to lie down on the spot where Brooke Lee, where she . . ."

"Died?" Wes asks incredulously.

"It was . . ." I shiver. "I don't know. He wasn't like that before. With me. He was nice. He was actually really nice and normal."

"Was he nice? Really? Because—" He stops, but I already know what he's going to say. I can hear it in his thoughts. "Can you keep a secret?"

I nod.

"Paige Wheeler and Lucas Hayes were together."

"They were?" I try to sound surprised.

"I saw them in those trees by the soccer field a couple of times. Kissing. They didn't see me." His lip curls.

"You look like you disapproved."

"Yeah, I did, sorta."

I shake my head. "Why did you even care?"

"I got the feeling that he'd talked her into keeping it a secret and . . ." He looks away. "I don't know. No way to treat a pretty girl."

"Pretty?" I say, my surprise becoming real.

His eyes narrow. "There's more types of pretty than yours, you know."

"Oh, no, that's not . . . I didn't mean it the way you think I meant it." *Kelsey*, I remind myself. *He thinks I'm Kelsey.*

He thinks I'm pretty, my mind counters, unbidden.

We walk back in silence across the field. I'm aware of his shoulder next to mine, his swinging arm, the rise and fall of his walk. I'm aware of the amount of space between us, mere inches. Just before we reach the school building, I stop. He stops, too.

"Hey," I say.

"Hey," he replies. He looks at me, squinting. "You're different."

"Different how?"

"From how I thought you'd be."

You are, too, I think, but instead I blurt out, "Would you go to prom with me?"

He blinks. "Didn't you already ask me that?"

"No," I say. "That wasn't me."

"An imposter, then?"

"Yes," I agree. "An imposter. But this is me right now. Asking you. To prom."

For a long moment, Wes doesn't say anything. Then, inch by inch, one side of his mouth lifts into a grin.

19: SECRET GIRLFRIEND

I STAY IN KELSEY FOR THE REST OF THE AFTERNOON. WES AND I arrive late in the art room to stunned silence from our classmates. No whispers, though, no laughs. I almost smile in gratitude. We sit at our usual opposite tables, not looking at each other, but after class, he falls in step with me again, walking me all the way to physics, the halls around us holding their breath.

He doesn't mention the prom until just before we part ways, when he runs a hand through his shaggy hair and says, "I seem to remember you saying that I don't have to get a corsage."

"No corsage necessary. And," I think quickly, "you don't have to pick me up. We can meet here at school. In the hall by that sheet for the mural."

"No meeting parents either?" He grins. "I didn't realize I was going to get lucky." The grin disappears as he hears his own words. "Oh. I mean . . . I didn't mean—"

I laugh until the embarrassment on his face becomes laughter, too.

"So, prom?" he says.

"So, prom," I agree, the words—no less who I am, no less the person I'm speaking them to—surreal.

I sit through physics in a daze. But beneath the disbelief is a little green sprout of happiness, like the ivy in the crevice of the roof ledge. But with it comes another feeling: regret as wide and deep as those first days after my death. What if I hadn't wasted my time—my*self*—on a guy who was only around for kisses in the trees? Would I have noticed the crooked-smiled burner who wanted to know me better? What if I hadn't pushed him away with my nicknames and judgments? Who would he have turned out to be? Who would I have been?

It's the memory of Lucas and the burner girl that finally pierces my fog. When the last bell rings, I walk Kelsey out to the road and then descend from my death spot to Mr. Fisk's classroom, where I stutter through the strange story of Lucas and the burner girl in the bathroom to the increasingly appalled expression on Evan's face.

"We have to tell Brooke," Evan says. "Where do you think she is? Maybe the gym? The soccer field?"

"I don't think we should say anything," I protest, well aware of all the other secrets I've been keeping from Evan, too. "Brooke already hates Lucas. This will just make it worse."

"But what if he does it again? What if she walks in on it? If he's doing it on her death spot, it's only a matter of time before she does."

And he's right, I know, but just when I gather the words to argue some more anyway, a voice behind us says, "Save your ethical debate."

The two of us turn to find Brooke in the doorway.

"I already walked in on him," she says.

"You saw? You mean, Lucas and—"

"His latest disposable girl?" She makes an angry, ugly scoffing sound. "Yeah, I saw."

"I'm sorry," I say.

"Don't *you* apologize for Lucas Hayes. And"—she pauses as if deciding something—"don't be angry at me." Her mouth twists. "Or, on second thought, *be* angry at me. I would."

I shake my head. "Why would I be angry at you?"

"Because." Brooke's gaze is so level and still, it's almost like she's forcing herself to meet my eyes. "Because I should have told you a long time ago."

"Told me what?"

She bites her lip. Unbites. "About Lucas Hayes and me."

"I don't understand," I say.

But this is a lie. I do understand. I've understood since I saw Lucas with the burner girl. I've understood from the moment he pointed to Brooke's death spot and asked her to lie down. Maybe part of me understood before that. The meeting with Heath. The flooding of Brooke's bathroom. *Don't say that*, Lucas had said to me in the burners' circle when I'd told him he'd practically saved a girl's life. *Because I didn't save her*, he'd said.

"You were together," I say slowly.

Brooke nods, her face coldly pretty, the way sharp things are, glittering, daring you to touch them. "We met up. Like you. We hooked up. Like you. If anyone else was around, he would ignore me. Like you."

Like you, her words whisper in my mind. *Like you*. "How long?" I say, and my voice sounds like an echo in my ears.

"From the end of junior year until the day I died. He didn't want anyone to know, though, and so no one did. I can keep a secret." Her mouth quirks. "Like you."

"And that day? The day you died?" Evan asks.

"It was Lucas, wasn't it?" I say, thinking of the conversation I overheard between him and Heath in the bathroom. "He was the one who bought the cocaine. Who wanted to use it."

"Did he get you to try it, too?" she asks.

"No."

"I'm surprised. But it was probably just a matter of time. He has a real nose for it, you know?" She wraps her ponytail around and around her hand, then unwraps it. Wraps it and unwraps it, like a boxer wrapping his fists. "I'll be honest. He didn't have to convince me much. I wanted to try it. We did it a couple of times together, after school, one weekend. That afternoon, we were supposed to go to his house because his mom was at work. But then Bosworth was monitoring the parking lot, so we couldn't get out, and who cares anyway, right? We'd just do it there in the bathroom and find our way off campus once Bosworth left." She pulls her ponytail across her face, hiding the crumple of her mouth and chin. "He handed it to me, you know that? Said, *You first*. And maybe something was wrong with it. Maybe something was wrong with me. I don't know, but it started to burn. My whole brain was burning. My eyes." She closes her eyes and exhales a shuddering breath. "And he watched it happen. He stood there staring while I died."

"And, when they found you, he said he didn't know you." I say the rest for her, the story everyone at the school knows. "He said he'd been walking by and heard a noise, like someone had fallen, and he'd gone in and found you on the floor."

"Innocent bystander," she says, eyes narrowing. "Big hero. Who wouldn't believe him? Everyone knew the kind of girl I was. No one even questioned it."

"He must have been scared," Evan says, "to lie like that."

"It doesn't matter," I say, and I'm surprised at the vehemence in my voice. "It doesn't matter if he was scared or in trouble or what. He should have said that he was there with her. He should have said that they were there together. He shouldn't have said he didn't know her, that she was just some girl."

20: THE DROP CLOTH

I MAKE A NEW PLAN THE NEXT DAY TO FOLLOW LUCAS HAYES
until he thinks of me. I will walk into Bosworth's office and make
Lucas tell the truth about his part in Brooke's death. And Lucas
won't be able to take it back later because I'll tell Bosworth to question Heath; I'll tell him to call Lucas's parents right then and there so
that I can confess to them, too. It's the truth. They'll have to believe it.

But the next morning, Lucas doesn't come to school. And when
Kelsey and Wes saunter in from the parking lot, their shoulders
bumping lightly as their steps fall together, I find myself following them instead, straining to hear the hum of their conversation, a
tremor in my middle.

Neither Kelsey nor Wes thinks of me that morning. They find
each other during passing breaks and take their lunches out to the
courtyard. They sit close on the flagstones, sharing body heat. I
watch them through the windows from inside the school. It's too
cold out there, even for a dead girl who can no longer feel things

like cold. Wes makes a comment that causes Kelsey to throw her head back and laugh. Would she be able to make him laugh? Yesterday, I had.

I step through the brick and glass out into the courtyard.

". . . sit inside with your friends?" Wes is saying when I get in earshot.

Kelsey makes a face. "No thanks."

"You're in a fight?" Wes asks.

"No fight. We're just not friends." Kelsey picks up a piece of foil from her lunch, adjusts it so that it makes a reflection on the flagstones. "I did some things. I don't know why. They were just little things, like wearing the wrong kind of clothes."

"Or asking the wrong kind of guy to the dance?" Wes raises an eyebrow.

She smiles down at her foil, makes the reflection dance.

My little things, I think. *The things I made her do.*

"At first it was just an impulse, an experiment. And it was like they thought I was someone else entirely. Some stranger. I was sure I'd ruined everything, my friendships, my entire senior year, myself. But then"—she squints—"I started to be okay with it. I started even to like it. I didn't have to be so careful to be nice and pretty and just this way. I could just . . ." She flips the foil onto the flagstones, where it joins with its reflection. "Be."

After lunch, art class takes the two of them past the drop cloth for my old mural. They glance at it, my name spoken in unison by their thoughts. Before I've thought about it, I'm pushing my way into Kelsey and blinking up at Wes through her hazel eyes. I reach out to take his hand, but have to pull back because he's still gazing at the drop cloth, his mind whispering, *Paige.*

"What are you thinking about?" I ask him.

"Oh," his eyes flick to me, back to the drop cloth. "Her, I guess. Paige Wheeler."

"You knew her?"

"Just a little."

My gaze falls on the sketchbook tucked under his arm. "Why did you draw all those pictures of her, then?"

He turns, nakedly surprised, my name gone from his thoughts mid-syllable, as if it has dropped through a trapdoor. "You saw those?"

"You drew them because she died?"

"Actually I drew these *before* she died. Or before I knew, anyway. I drew them that afternoon. Seventh period."

"When she fell," I whisper.

He offers me the sketchbook. I take it gingerly, flip through the pages, my face appearing before me again and again, but with small differences between each drawing, as if I'm changing my expression, as if I'm moving. That girl who is me. Who isn't me.

"Why did you draw them?" I ask again.

"I don't know. Maybe I liked her."

I'm standing on tile floor, hard and cold and square beneath my feet, but suddenly it feels like I can't count on the ground at all. It's like my first days learning to hover, when the floor was an iced-over lake—one wrong step, and I'll fall through.

"Maybe?" I hear my voice say.

"All right, not maybe. I liked her."

"You should have told her."

Wes smiles humorlessly. "Well, what do you know? I did."

"No, you didn't."

He raises his eyebrows.

"I mean, are you sure you did? Because I don't think—"

"I made it pretty clear."

Had he? I think back to the smirks that might have been smiles, the mockery that might have been flirtation. And then, there was that moment in the burners' circle. *If you were meeting me*, he'd said, *I'd make a point of being here.*

And what had I said to that ridiculous burner, that annoying joker who was Wes Nolan? *I'd make a point of losing track of time.*

That's what I'd said.

All my time is gone now. I won't get to chart the crookedness of another boy's smile. I won't get to leap giddily from teasing gibe to gibe. I won't get to walk down the hallway with him like Kelsey did today, everyone noting, *They're together. Those two.* I won't get to fall in love. I've never been in love.

I turn to Wes and ask the question I don't want to ask, the question I have no right to ask, the question that I'm already asking: "If you liked her, if you liked Paige, what are you doing here with me?"

"Kelsey," he says, and I'm surprised by how the sound of her name on his tongue suddenly hurts me. "Whatever it was, it doesn't matter anymore."

"That's right. She's dead now."

Wes reaches out, and I take a step back, his fingers grazing the place where I'd been. This time, the problem isn't that he's thinking my name, but that he isn't.

"I can't—" I say, and I don't know how to finish. I can't what? What is it that I can't do with Wes?

Besides nothing.

Besides anything.

I turn and walk away from the hurt in his eyes, the light in her eyes, too, that girl under the tree.

. . .

As I march Kelsey out of the school and across the parking lot, here are the things I don't care about: I don't care that I'm making Kelsey skip class. I don't care that I made her break things off with Wes. I don't care that she might like him. I don't care that he might like her back. I don't care that he's not following me. Her. Whoever. I don't care that he might have liked me. I don't care about him. I don't care about myself.

I'm walking faster and faster in Kelsey's tippy-top boots, until she's across the road and I'm back where I belong, up on the school roof. The parking lot stretches out in front of me. One time, not so long ago, it must have been a field, not a parking lot. What happens to the grass when they lay all that tar over it?

I'll tell you what happens.

It dies.

I stare down at the blacktop.

Something catches my eye.

A movement.

Something.

Nothing.

I blink.

Harriet Greene.

There she is, right down there in the parking lot. She stands on the accident site, at the end of the curling tire tracks. She looks around her, bewildered, turns in a slow circle.

"Harriet!" I shout.

Then, she's gone.

Blink again and she's back. This time, though, she's flickering, like a guttering candle. She's there, then not, there, not.

There.

I glance over my shoulder, taking in the distance back across the roof, back to the door, down through the school. She could disappear again any moment. There's not time to get down there, not time for the stairs.

I take a shaking breath and step up on the ledge.

I don't look down at the ground below me. I know what I'll see if I do, that little patch of tar darker than the rest. Instead, I steel myself. Instead, I do what they all said I did.

I jump.

This time, I'm awake for the fall. Each set of windows I pass blazes with reflected light, like a flashbulb. I have enough time to think, *Thirty-two feet per second squared*, before I land in a heap, the ground jarring up through whatever part of me has been left in this world. I stand, but find I can't manage to hover, not after the shock of that fall. I limp forward, toes skimming through the asphalt. Harriet is still there in front of me (thank God), only yards away.

She's seen me now. She's shouting something. But the volume is turned off. I can see her, but there's no sound.

I wave my arms, gesture to my ears. "Harriet! I can't hear you!"

Her silent shouts become more frantic. She points back at the school, then at herself. I'm almost there, close enough to see that she's saying the same thing over and over, but she's flickering again, and I can't make out the word her lips are forming.

Then she's gone.

I stand at the end of the tire tracks, follow them with my eyes as they curl into nothing.

21. SOMEONE ELSE'S DAUGHTER

EVAN, BROOKE, AND I SIT IN A ROW IN FRONT OF HARRIET'S accident site for the rest of the afternoon.

Evan turns to me. "You're sure you don't know what she was trying to say?"

"I was too far away. It was the same thing, though. The same word or two words. And, like I told you, she pointed to the school, then to herself."

Evan frowns.

"What is it?" I ask.

"Something's been bothering me," he says. "You know it's just been me here for . . . a while."

"How long?" Brooke asks.

"Years," Evan admits.

"Decades?" I whisper.

He looks down. "A while," he repeats. "And that makes sense because it's a school. No one's supposed to die in high school."

I feel a twinge as he says this. It's true. I look around at the three of us. We weren't supposed to die so young. "But then there was Brooke," I say, "and me, and now maybe Harriet."

"All in the same year," Brooke finishes.

"It's like they say," Evan traces over the tire tracks with his finger, "this place is cursed."

I still fully intend to make Lucas admit the truth to Principal Bosworth, but he doesn't show up the next day either. Only half of the upperclassmen show anyway because prom is tonight. It's tradition to spend the morning sleeping in, the afternoon getting sandblasted and shellacked at the salon.

I hang out in the main office, waiting for a call about Harriet. I expect Evan and Brooke to be there, too, but this morning it's just me. Bosworth and Mrs. Morello are both shut up in his office, and the secretary is playing solitaire on the computer, no calls ringing. Twenty minutes later, Kelsey Pope slinks into the office, hair in wet ropes, features faint without their usual makeup. I'm surprised she's here at school and not at home readying herself for the dance.

"Can I get a late pass?" she asks the secretary.

While the secretary bends to get the form, Kelsey picks up a flyer from the front counter, fiddling with it. I think of the origami flower she folded at my grief group meeting. Just then, the office door opens and Bosworth ushers out the people from his meeting.

Those people are my parents.

My mother emerges first, purse wrapped tightly under her arm. My father follows, his hand set on her shoulder, as if this small touch is necessary to their forward momentum, though I can't tell if he is guiding her or she is leading him out the door.

". . . for coming in today, Mr. and Mrs. Wheeler," Bosworth is saying.

At the sound of their name, Kelsey thinks of me, *Paige*. Without a thought, I step into her, and thankfully, she doesn't resist.

My mother is buttoning up a dark jacket that I've never seen before; she must have bought it new for spring. My father reluctantly takes Bosworth's offered hand, giving it a tepid shake. I scan them for other differences, new wrinkles, dark circles, white hairs, but it's like trying to think about your parents by their given names instead of *Mom* and *Dad*. I can't see anything except that they're overwhelmingly my parents right there in front of me. They're my parents walking past me out the office door. They're my parents who might leave this school, never to come back.

"Wait!" I shout.

Everyone looks at me. My mother has a polite expression on her face, as if she doesn't even know me. Which she doesn't, I remind myself. And I decide that I'd exchange all of Kelsey's beauty in a second to look like my mother's daughter right now.

"Wait," I repeat. I take a tripping step toward my mom.

She raises her eyebrows, forehead wrinkling.

I have no idea what to say. I look down at Kelsey's hands, still holding the half-folded flyer. I scan its heading and thrust it forward. "You should come to the spaghetti dinner next week."

"Oh," my mother says faintly.

"It's to raise money for the jazz band."

"Kelsey," Bosworth warns. "These are—"

"It's a really good cause," I talk over him. "Music and the arts and education, and lots of people come to it, parents come to it," I finish lamely.

"I think that's enough for now," Bosworth says.

But my mother steps past him and takes the flyer from me. "Maybe we will come. I like music." She smiles briefly. "Thank you for telling us about this, . . . ?" She waits for my name.

"Kelsey," I say. I hold the paper for as long as I can without keeping it from her, and then I let it slide through my fingers. She takes it, running her hand over it to smooth the creases away.

I follow my parents out of the office, pretending to bend over the drinking fountain so that I can keep watching them. They grow smaller and smaller down the hall.

When I can't see them anymore, I walk to the social studies hall and stand at the window set into the door of Mr. Pon's classroom as one and another and another of the kids notice me, all of them smirking at the sight of my face peering in. Finally, one of them takes pity on me and nudges Wes Nolan. When Wes looks up from his textbook, I'm praying that his expression won't be angry. And it isn't. He raises his hand and calls the teacher's name.

When we find an empty classroom, shutting the door behind us, I step forward and, before he can say anything, I say, "You can kiss me."

"Kelsey."

"What?"

"I think we should talk about—"

"I don't care. I don't care if you think of her."

"Her?" he says, then blanches. "Oh, no. No. I wouldn't pretend that you're, I wouldn't imagine that you're . . ." *Paige*, his mind whispers, even if he won't say it.

But that was not what I meant. Actually, I meant the opposite. I meant that I don't care if he thinks of Kelsey when he's kissing me.

"You can hold me," I say. "Maybe right now you can just hold me."

He nods. "Okay. That'd be okay."

His coat smells like cigarettes, his chin rests on the top of my head in Kelsey's damp hair. His hands don't rub my back consolingly, but just hold me, like the earth holds me when I set my feet on it. He doesn't think my name again. He doesn't think *Paige*. But I meant it. I don't care.

22. PROM NIGHT

WHAT WOULD I HAVE WORN TO PROM?

I'd been to only two school dances freshman year before Usha and I had decided that they were stupid, so I have only two dresses in my closet at home: red and black. The black one is short; the red one is red. Getting ready for those other dances, I'd stand naked in my bedroom, hair wet on my back, and lay both dresses on the bed, trying to imagine how my night would be different if I wore one or the other. Red dress or black? Hair piled on my head or tousled? Dewy cheek and lip gloss or shadowed bedroom eyes? It didn't matter. I was never the girl in my head.

Tonight, I wonder where those two dresses are now. Are they still hanging in my closet like promises never meant to be kept? Or have they been folded up and closed in a box with my name on it? Or maybe they've been donated to charity and are being worn right now by two other girls at two other proms, with entirely different boys and entirely different songs, their dance moves making entirely different patterns of wrinkles in the fabric.

Kelsey arrives early, just after the chaperones, and leans against the wall opposite from the drop cloth. She wears a knee-length shift with straps so thin they look like they're made to be snapped. The fabric has been woven through with keen silver threads so that the dress winks dangerously, like a thousand needles, as she turns. She surveys the empty hallway once more, and now certain that Wes isn't there, she steps back against the wall to wait. Stray strands of her hair, brushed into a frantic shine, begin to climb above her head, tiny static snakes against the brick. I remember a page I'd read in one of the left-open library books, how in actual mythology, Medusa didn't turn you into stone because she was so ugly, but because she was so beautiful, and because you were fool enough to meet her eye.

I draw closer, peering at Kelsey's face. We both turn at a spike of laughter from people passing the mouth of the hallway, faces stuck in smiles at seeing Kelsey Pope alone at the dance. Kelsey presses a hand to her cheek self-consciously.

"You look beautiful," I say, not sure whether I'm saying it to apologize or simply because it's true. As if in answer, Kelsey's mind whispers, *Paige*. There's no more resistance than breaking the skin of a pool as I step into her waiting form, and now I am beautiful, too.

I post myself at the mouth of the hall, watching the dancegoers clump in twos, fours, groups. They all spare looks for me, most of them turning away, expressions laced with laughter.

Then, Lucas Hayes lopes down the hall, the little dark-mouthed burner girl tucked under his arm. I goggle at them. Lucas wouldn't have taken Brooke to prom—not me either. What does it mean that he's brought her? A gang of paired ponies and testos come after Lucas, the ponies dropping behind their dates, not sure whether to stare at Lucas Hayes and his low-rent date or at Kelsey Pope and her no-date.

But then there he is, my date, Wes Nolan. He shoulders past them, already muttering apologies. He halts, excuses fading out. "You look . . . shit." He shakes his head. "You'll hate it if I say 'beautiful.'"

"You can say it."

"All right."

Wes grins. We grin at each other like goons.

"Well, say it if you're going to say it, then."

"You look beautiful," he says, no grin.

A chord rises in me that is both the swell of the music and the pain of the string being plucked.

"Not me."

"Who else but you?"

When he grabs my hand, I let him take it.

I have never danced like this. But it's how I would've liked to dance. Wes and I leap; we twist and spin. It's weird. It's fun. A circle forms around us. With my eye makeup blurring and my hair whipping and Wes laughing in my ear, I can't tell if they're admirers or jeerers. Then I think, *Does it matter?* During the slow songs, I let Wes wrap his arms around me tight, like I'm impossible to break, like I'm invincible. Even the chaperones don't dare approach us.

Partway through the dance, I see Evan standing in a corner among the wallflowers. I follow his gaze and find Mr. Fisk presiding over the refreshments table. Something must cross my face because Wes touches my arm and says, "Just ignore him."

He nods past Evan and Mr. Fisk to Lucas Hayes, who cuts through the gym, threshing the crowd. The burner girl follows after him in a dress as dark and brief as her lips. Lucas turns and says something to her; the words are short. She stops at this comment, all the sass draining from her, her hands falling to her sides. Lucas walks on, leaving her behind. The crowd flails around her, buffeting her left and right, until she washes up by the refreshments table. When Lucas reaches the door to the hall, he looks back. Somehow, across the gym full of dancers, his eyes catch mine and hold them. They don't look like his eyes, charmingly lazy and warm. His eyes look suspicious, mean. He darts out the door.

Through the doorway Lucas has just left, Usha enters, wearing a pouf of canary tulle that we'd found together at a garage sale a year ago. A group of people surround her—biblicals, well-rounders, even a pony or two—though none are nearly so vividly arrayed. One of them reaches to touch the hem of Usha's skirt with a look of unguarded admiration. Usha laughs and spins, the yellow fanning out. Usha is a twirling type of girl again.

"We have to vote!" I remember.

"Vote?" Wes asks.

"For prom queen."

"That's right. You're nominated."

"I forgot," I say, lifting a hand to my forehead.

"Really?" Wes asks. "You *forgot*."

"Actually, I did. But it doesn't matter. I'm going to vote for Usha Das."

"Well, I'm going to vote for you." He grins.

"If you must," I say, and lead the way to the table with the ballot box. Mrs. Morello hands us the slips of paper. At the last minute,

I change my mind and make a check not next to *Usha Das,* but *Kelsey Pope*. Consider it my apology. I fold the paper and drop it in the box with a smile.

Still, I'm just as happy when Usha is called up to the makeshift stage and crowned prom queen. She's fumbling with the hairpins, and I'm clapping and cheering louder than anyone else. Wes musses my hair and swings his arm around my shoulder, murmuring, "No one has any idea how cool you really are," and this compliment I claim as my own.

We escape the heat and noise, ending up back in the hallway, the dance still in full swing. The song lyrics from the past few hours echo in my ears like someone is whispering them to me from another room. Wes walks backward in front of me, his shirt unbuttoned at the collar, his tie laid carelessly over one shoulder, and his cheeks flushed pink all the way to his ears.

I reach out and let my fingers graze his jaw. He tries to catch them, but I'm too quick, and his hand closes on air.

I step over to the drop cloth. "Why do they still have this up?"

"I think it's to protect the mural until it's done."

"But there's no mural."

"What do you mean? It's right under there."

I feel Kelsey's pulse in my neck and wrists, starting up a flutter faster than when I was dancing. I pinch the edge of the drop cloth, the warp and weft of the fabric between my fingers. "No, I saw. Usha painted over it. It's just a blank wall now."

Wes shakes his head. "It's a mural. She's been working on it for over a month."

Then I remember something: Stumbling down the hall after I'd seen Lucas with the burner girl, I almost ran into her, Usha up on her ladder. I'd been so upset that it hadn't registered. I press a hand to my neck. There it is, my pulse, a little under-the-skin creature beating its wings.

"She kept painting it?"

"Of course."

"But I saw her painting over it. She said, 'Maybe we should be trying to forget.'"

"Here. See?" Wes steps past me and yanks the drop cloth free. My eyes follow it as it floats gently to the floor.

I don't look at the mural right away. First, I look at Wes looking at it. He scans the wall, floor to ceiling, his eyes lit up like they were when he broke through the trees to the burners' circle and found me scratching my designs into the ground.

"Will you look at that?" he says, voice awed.

So I look.

The mural reaches from floor to ceiling, a maze of lines and curves. Birds.

The flocks of birds from Usha's notebook, not inked centimeters across, but painted meters high, beaks pointed, wingspans unfurled, feathers all colors and speckles, delicate necks stretched toward the sky. And, parachutes, the calmly floating parachutes, their passengers tied safely below. Airplanes with whirring propellers. Bunches of helium balloons, hot-air balloons, too, with wicker riding baskets. Clouds of insects—monarchs, wasps, bluebottles, and dragonflies. Dragons, griffins, other impossible creatures, flying horses, and angels with trumpets as slender as their wrists. And there at the bottom, tiny in its corner, my contribution to the mural, my fuzzy little moth.

Usha has painted things that can't fall.

She's painted things that can fly.

I feel it again, that dissolving feeling, the feeling that happens whenever I inhabit someone. But this time it's different, stronger, warmer . . . wider? And then I hear the voices, dozens of them, a whole crowd, whispering to one another. I can't make out the words, but the tone is warm, like how you might whisper *I love you* to someone who's sleeping. I place my palm against the slick shine of the dried paint, the tiny furrows of brushstroke, the wall beneath. The wall that will last for years.

"Hey," Wes says softly.

I turn to face him.

"Hey," he says again, taking one of my hands in both of his and holding it to his chest. "Why are you crying?"

"Because." I shake my head. "Because I feel alive."

Wes leans down and kisses me. I kiss him back. His lips taste like cigarettes, like paper burnt until it's cinders, but then the cinders glow softly, rekindling with the warmth of his mouth. After seconds and years and eons, we part.

He grins, and I let out a little burst of laughter.

"So that was funny to you?" Wes says, but he's still grinning.

I shake my head. "What are you even doing here, Wes Nolan?"

"Nothing much," he says, "Just being here. With you."

Footfalls behind us. We break apart, and Usha stands there in her dandelion of a dress, lipstick on her front teeth, rhinestone crown pulling away from the pins that hold it to her hair. She looks perfect, by the way.

"Sorry," she mutters, backing away.

"Usha!" I call.

She turns, an uncertain expression on her face.

"You painted this." I point at the mural.

"You shouldn't have taken that off." She gestures at the crumpled drop cloth. "It's not ready yet. I still haven't really—"

"Thank you," I interrupt.

"For what?"

"They're flying," I say.

She nods.

"Now people will remember her as something other than . . . I . . . I'm sorry that I lied, that I said she jumped."

Usha's brows draw together. She pulls the crown from her head, holds it in her hands, running her fingers over the fake gemstones. "You don't have to pretend."

"I'm not pretending." I put a hand to my chest. "I really am sorry. I'm sorry I lied."

"You don't have to pretend to . . . I know it wasn't a lie." Usha looks up from her crown. "Paige stepped off the roof."

"Usha. *No.*" My hands fall to my sides, the silky fabric of Kelsey's dress in them, crumpling and uncrumpling in my fists. "I know what people have been saying, but it's not true. She fell. *She fell.*"

Usha doesn't shake her head, she doesn't raise her voice, she doesn't argue. She simply says, "Paige stepped off the roof. I saw her. Everyone else was looking the other way, at those boys throwing things. But I was looking at her. And you were, too. You screamed. When she did it, you screamed, and everyone else looked. You don't have to pretend. I saw it. I saw you see it."

"But no," I argue. "That's impossible, because I—she— didn't jump."

"Kelsey," Wes says, "maybe right now isn't—"

My mind latches on to something. Usha and my conversation at the lunch table. "You said, you told Jenny, that I shouldn't have said it, that I shouldn't have said that Paige jumped."

"I was mad that you told everyone, not because it was a lie, but because it was true." Usha looks down at her crown, pulls free a strand of hair that was caught between the stones. When she looks up again, her expression is peaceful. "I'm not mad anymore. I was carrying it around, that secret, and it was *hurting* me. But after you said it, after everyone knew, I told my mom and we talked about it. I forgave you. And I painted. And I forgave her, too."

I open my mouth, "But she couldn't have jumped, she just, she turned and then—"

"She jumped," Usha says, plain and soft. "She did."

I start to say *no, no way, you're wrong*, but I can't say any of it because I'm falling all over again. Kelsey is slowly and firmly pushing me out of her body, and I can't find my hold on her, can't even find my feet. I'm sinking through the floor. I see a flash of the three of them—Wes, Kelsey, and Usha standing in a circle—before the floor takes me.

I land in the basement in a heap on my side. This time I don't have the strength to get up. I draw my knees to my chest, rest my head in their valley, and listen to the ghost frogs singing softly around me.

23: HOW EVAN DIED

"PAIGE," A VOICE SAYS SOFTLY. "PAIGE," IT SAYS AGAIN.

I can hear the music of the dance, faintly, from the gym up above. The dance is still going on, then.

"Paige," the voice repeats.

I raise my head reluctantly.

Evan crouches in front of me. "What are you doing down here?"

"I fell through. I—" I choke on my words.

"What is it?"

I shake my head, dirt pressing against my cheek.

Just like in the grave.

"Here. Sit up," Evan says.

I follow his instructions like a child. We sit in silence, Evan watching me steadily, until finally I manage to say, "Did I kill myself?"

Evan's eyebrows shoot up. "No. You've always said that—"

"Because Usha said I did."

"But those were rumors—" Evan begins.

"She said she *saw* it. That Kelsey saw it, too." I swallow. "Usha wouldn't lie. I thought Kelsey was lying about me, but it was the truth."

"Are you sure?"

"I don't know. I don't remember it like that. And I don't know why I would—no—I know that I *wouldn't* do that. Not to Usha or to my parents. Or to myself. I wouldn't hurt them. I wouldn't be so selfish, so unfair to—"

Evan turns away from me, drops his head into his hands.

"Evan? What did I say? What is it?"

He raises his face, his expression pained. The music from the gym winds in, snaking itself around the two of us. Slowly, Evan points to the ceiling. "I died up there, you know."

"In the gym," I say. "I know."

"Seventeen years ago."

I glance at his clothes, and he catches it. "Fashions change. And then they change back. Someone once said the only constant is change."

"Who was that?"

"Heraclitus. Ancient philosopher."

"Sometimes I think nothing changes," I say.

"There's a quote for that, too."

"Right. 'The more things change, the more they stay the same.'"

"*Plus ça change, plus c'est la même chose,*" he recites.

"Show-off."

"Sorry." His smile looks like a stranger that has accidentally wandered onto his sad face. "Seventeen years of French class."

"How did you die?"

"I killed myself."

"Oh."

"I snuck in at night with the gun from my parents' safe. They kept it locked, but I'd figured out the combination years before.

"There'd been a basketball game, and so the floor was just washed and the doors were open for it to dry. That's how I got in. I took it as a sign. The janitor was on the other side of the building. I could hear the radio. And I thought, *He'll be the only one to hear the shot. He'll be the one to find me.* I tried to remember what he looked like so that I could picture him, his face, but then I remembered that he was the night janitor, and so I'd never even seen him. I imagined him anyway. I pictured my grandfather with a thick white moustache, holding a wet mop.

"Then I thought, *Every day he cleans up after kids, and now he can clean up an actual kid.* Do you think that's funny?"

"No. That's not funny," I say.

"I took my shoes off to walk across the floor, so I wouldn't mess up how he'd washed it, and *that* seemed funny. I couldn't laugh, though, because it's . . . Did you ever notice that it's harder to laugh when you're alone?"

I nod.

"I put my shoes back on when I got to the seal. I didn't want to die in my socks. I'd thought I was going to put the gun in my mouth, but then when I was there, I didn't want to have to, you know, taste the metal."

"Evan," I murmur, but I don't have anything good to say after that. Or anything at all. So, he keeps talking, his eyes fixed on the dirt floor.

"I put the gun to my temple instead. And I stood there. I stood there for a long time, so long my arm got tired, and I had to rest it. It was heavy. Guns are heavy. I thought about just going home. But then it would be the same, wouldn't it? The next week and the next and the rest of my life, really. Because it wasn't going to go away, even after I graduated and got away from Paul Revere, *I'd* still be the same. The more things change, the more they stay the same. And, if my father ever found out—"

"There's nothing wrong with you," I say, wishing that I could've said this seventeen years ago to the boy in the gym.

"Thank you." He looks at me. "I know that now. I mean, I *believe* it now. Did you do the math? I'd be thirty-four years old. I guess I *am* thirty-four years old. I've had as much death as I did life. That's a long time to learn a lesson."

I reach out across the floor and put my hand through Evan's. "Tell me the rest."

"There's not much left to tell. I lifted the gun again, and I pulled the trigger."

I close my eyes and hear the crack of the shot, a sound louder than a gym full of cheering students. In the gym's empty center, I see a shadow-thin boy falling to the floor. Then I force my eyes open, because Evan has never looked away from me.

"I woke up a few days later, I guess. At first I didn't know where I was, some basement, but then I heard them up above me, sneakers squeaking, boys shouting to pass the ball. Gym class." Evan smiles wryly. "I was trying to escape high school, and I ended up right back in it."

"What did you do next?"

"A lot of freaking out. The school had covered up the fact that there was a suicide in the gym, the entire fact that it was a suicide, for that matter. No one talked about it, actually. It was like I'd just disappeared.

"For a while, I followed the night janitor, who turned out to be not my grandpa, of course, but this little Dominican woman. She talked to herself, and so I'd fill in the gaps in her conversation. Sometimes her responses would fit what I'd just said. I still think maybe she could—not hear me, but who knows? She retired ten years ago.

"I followed my friends around, too, watched them graduate. This one guy, I was in love with him, but he was so popular and so much a guy's guy. Sometimes I suspected that he might feel . . . but I was never brave enough to ask." He pauses. "Then, just a couple years ago, he came back and started teaching here."

"Mr. Fisk." I can tell by Evan's face that I'm right. "That's why you sit in his class? Evan, he's the adviser for those meetings I told you about where gay kids—"

"I know. A couple weeks ago, I heard him talking to a student about that group."

Me, I think. That student talking to Mr. Fisk was me pretending to be Chris Rackham.

"He said he'd had a friend, and I heard it. I heard him think my name."

"You did?"

"I lost my hover. I dropped right through the floor."

I remember turning to find Evan's cupboard empty. I'd thought he'd left the room, that he hadn't heard any of it.

"I went to one of those meetings. Those kids. It's not perfect, but . . ." He pauses and looks into the dark of the basement. "I take it back. Things do change."

"Do you think Mr. Fisk could be gay?"

He laughs. "If you only knew the hours I once spent asking myself that question." He shakes his head ruefully. "But it doesn't really matter, does it? What matters is that he considered me a friend. That he . . ." Evan's voice, steady through the whole story, begins to shake now. "That he remembers me."

We listen to the noises of the dance above us, the thrum of the bass, the tangle of voices.

"Ask me if I regret it," Evan says.

"I don't have to ask that."

"Do it anyway. Please. I want to be able to say it."

"Okay. Do you regret it?"

"Every day. Every day of my life." He smiles at the word *life*.

"There's something I have to tell you. And I don't know if I can."

"After what I just told you?" Evan snorts. "You can. You better."

"Okay." I take a breath. "But please don't hate me." I explain everything I've been keeping secret from Evan, starting with the afternoon of the grief group meeting, when I thought I'd held Lucas Hayes's hand, ending with tonight in the hallway when Usha said she'd seen me step off the roof. Evan doesn't interrupt.

When I finish, I expect him to yell at me, but instead he squints. It's the faraway look he gets when he's solving a complex math problem in his head.

"You're angry," I say when I can't stand the silence anymore. "I'm sorry. I should have told you about the inhabitations, about everything."

He's still silent.

"It's just I knew what you'd say. You'd say that I shouldn't do it, that I didn't have the right." I expel a long breath. "And that's true. But I didn't want to stop because . . . Evan, I got to be alive again."

He finally breaks his silence, but he doesn't scold me, doesn't say anything about my explanation. Instead, he says, "Brooke."

"What?"

"We have to find Brooke."

"Why?" I say. "Evan?"

But he's already up and climbing the stairs to the school.

We can't find Brooke. She's not at the dance. She's not on her death spot. We resort to walking through the halls, poking our heads into empty classrooms, calling her name.

"Evan, what is this?" I ask him after we've cleared the entire art and music wing. "Why do we have to find Brooke?"

"I'll tell you later. I promise."

"Why not now?"

He bites his lip. "I want to be sure. Where should we look next?"

"Maybe outside," I suggest, leading Evan through the doors, out to the student parking lot. "Sometimes she hangs out on the—"

Evan goes stock-still.

I turn to see what he's looking at.

Harriet.

She's where I saw her before, crouched in the middle of the parking lot, on the site of her accident. We run to her, and this time we reach her before she disappears. She's speaking urgently again, the same word over and over. And again, we can't hear the sound of what she's saying.

"Can you make it out?" I ask Evan. "It's . . . Is it . . . ?" A chill goes through me.

Evan says it. "'Brooke.' She's saying 'Brooke.'"

"What does it mean? Is Brooke in trouble?"

"No," Evan says. "I think she's—"

"Evan." I gesture to Harriet, whose mouth has fallen open in fear. She points at something behind us. We turn.

"What?" Evan says. "The school?"

But I know where to look. I tilt my head up.

There, on the school roof, stands a figure, face tipped to the sky. A guy, I can tell that much. He doesn't stand up on the ledge—to my great relief—but on the flat of the roof. He peers over the ledge, though, as if assessing the drop to the ground. There's something familiar about him. "Is it . . . ?" I ask, then answer myself. "It's Lucas."

"No, it's not," Evan says.

"It is," I say. "I can tell. It's definitely Lucas Hayes."

"No. Paige. Look at Harriet. Look."

I turn back to Harriet, and she holds her arm out straight, a direct line, finger pointed. And it's obvious what she's pointing at: Lucas Hayes on the edge of the roof. But the thing is, she's still saying it, her lips are still forming the same one word: *Brooke.*

Then she winks out.

And Evan and I are left alone in the parking lot.

24: THE SCHOOL ROOF

"IT'S HER," EVAN SAYS, BOTH OF US GAZING UP AT THE FIGURE of Lucas on the school roof. "That's Brooke. She's possessed him."

Memories lay themselves out in my mind like a hand of playing cards, one flipped over, then the next: Lucas murmuring, *Yeah, right,* when Mrs. Morello had suggested he was upset about Brooke's death. Lucas standing in front of the overflowing sinks. *Karma, man. Sucks when it finally comes around again.* Lucas pointing to the spot on the tile, Brooke's death spot. *You should lie down on it.*

I knew something was different about him, different from the popular Lucas goofing with his friends, different too from the Lucas who'd met me in the trees. I explained it away as the drugs, the guilt, the grief, but really, it was Brooke. Lucas flooding the bathroom? Brooke. Lucas ordering the burner girl onto the floor? Brooke. Lucas climbing to the school roof? Brooke. She figured out how to inhabit people, just like I did.

"She's done it before," I say. Evan isn't looking up at the roof anymore. Now he's staring at me. I have the impulse to give him a good shove, because it's no good standing here gaping at each other, not when any minute Brooke could look down and see us. I duck between two parked cars, gesturing for him to follow me.

"We have to do something," I insist.

"Paige," he says.

"Don't you get it? She blames Lucas for her death. She hates him."

"Paige." He winces. "I'm so sorry."

"And now she's up there on the roof. She's going to make him jump. She's going to make him jump like . . ." I trail off. "Why are you sorry?"

Evan looks down.

"Why are you sorry?" I repeat.

Instead of answering, he asks, "What did you just say?"

"What did I . . ." I shake my head. "That Brooke hates Lucas. That if we don't do anything, she's going to make him jump off the roof."

"You said *like*."

I peek over the car at the roof. Lucas is standing just where he was before, looking over the ledge. "Evan. Come on. We have to do something."

"You said, 'She's going to make him jump *like* . . .'"

"Did I? So what?" But something is rising in me. I picture myself standing on the ledge of the roof, fragile egg held out in front of me, sky above me a muddy sheet. "She's going to make him jump off the roof like . . . I don't know."

"Like you?" Evan asks.

"No. That's not what I was going to say."

Evan repeats the sentence. "'She's going to make him jump *like . . . she made me*'?"

"I slipped," I tell him. "It was an accident. I *slipped*."

But had I?

I hadn't committed suicide. I knew that much.

But Usha said she'd seen me step off the roof, that Kelsey had seen it, too. And maybe Kelsey *had* seen it, because that's what she'd told people, that I'd jumped. Why would she say that? Why would both of them say it?

I picture it again: the roof. One of my feet stepping up onto the ledge, then the other. Mr. Cochran heading back to Lucas. Someone shouting *Catch!* The sound of the egg breaking. I'd started to turn because I'd decided that I was going to smile at him, even though I'd been chiding myself for smiling at him a moment before. *Like some no-respect burner girl*, I'd thought, *like poor, dead Brooke Lee.*

I'd thought of her.

I'd invited her in.

Horror rises in me, wider and giddier than the bleak gray sky. I'm falling again. I'm falling. Except I'm not; I'm still here, standing on the ground.

"It was her," I whisper. "Brooke. She inhabited me. She stepped off the roof."

"I'm sorry," Evan repeats. "I'm so sorry."

"But why? Why would she do that?"

"Because you were with Lucas?"

"You think she was jealous? You're wrong. She hated him."

"She hated him." Evan nods. "And so she could make him watch it all over again, his girlfriend dying."

"I wasn't his girlfriend," I reply automatically, thinking how ridiculous this now sounds. Then I think of something else. "When I was alive, Brooke was following me. Harriet told me."

Evan sucks in a breath. "Did she tell you that in front of Brooke?"

"Harriet!" I clap my hand over my mouth. "Do you think Brooke—"

"Made Harriet get into the accident?" Evan asks.

"She hit Heath Mineo," I say.

"Who sold Lucas the drugs she OD'd on," Evan finishes.

"Evan"—my voice breaks—"she *killed* me."

The weight of it hits me, and I curl up, wishing I could sink lower than the ground, down into the earth, down through the layers of sediment and silt and bedrock until my spirit puffs to ash in the Earth's core. It feels like maybe I could, if I wanted to enough.

Except I can't. Because even though Lucas was a coward, he doesn't deserve to die. Because Brooke could hurt someone else next, someone I care about, like Usha or Wes, or even someone I don't care about, some pious biblical or nodding pony or smug well-rounder. I don't want anyone else to be hurt. I want them to have a chance at life, even if I don't anymore. I want them to have a chance *because* I don't.

I stand.

And as I stand, Lucas steps, one foot after the other, onto the ledge of the roof.

"What are you doing?" Evan asks.

"I'm going to talk to her."

He scrambles up next to me. "We'll go together."

"No. Just me."

"Why?"

"Because I can get there quicker."

Evan looks from the school roof to the property line.

"Stay down here," I tell him. "In case . . ." I don't finish. *In case she jumps.*

He nods once. "Go."

But I'm already running.

At first, I see stars.

I've appeared on the roof, looking up at the night sky. I drop my gaze down. There, at my feet, is the crack in the cement where the little stem of ivy that I plucked weeks ago is trying to grow back. Then I gather all my courage and look along the edge of the roof.

There.

A few feet away from me, also up on the ledge, Lucas Hayes inches forward so that the scuffed toes of his dress shoes are over the edge. And I have no way to touch him, no way to pull him back.

"Brooke," I say, begging my voice not to wobble, "I know it's you."

Lucas turns in my direction. He might just be surveying the roof and the neighborhoods spread out to his right, but his eyes (Brooke looking out from behind them) catch on me before they scan by.

"I could do it," Lucas says, as if to himself. Even though the words come out in Lucas's deep drawl, it's Brooke saying them. And I know she's saying them to me. "I could jump."

"Don't," I say. "Please don't."

"After all *I* did, you have to admit, I deserve what I get." She looks right at me then, and her eyes are empty.

"You should get down," I say. I step down myself, onto the roof, and walk in a slow half circle until I'm on the other side of her (him? them?).

"You hate him," I tell her. "Fine. Okay. I understand about hate because I hate you. I hate you for what you did to me."

She twitches at this.

"You took my life away. *My whole life.*" My voice shakes. "But I'm still up here trying to save you anyway."

"Him," she mutters. "You're trying to save him."

"You," I insist. "Both of you."

I reach out to her, palm up.

She looks at my hand, and I almost think she's going to step onto the roof with me. But just then, Evan's voice sails up from the parking lot. "Paige! The dance is ending!" And Brooke's expression on Lucas's face hardens into a mask.

"You can't touch me," she says, and shuffles back along the ledge.

I take another step forward, arm still extended. She takes another step back. The heel of Lucas's shoe hits up against the crack in the roof's ledge, stopping her, the little shoot of ivy peeking out from under his sole. She looks at the ground below, then back at me.

"They'll be here soon," she says.

She's right. They will. The two of us pause in the moment of silence before the noise. Then the gym doors rattle open, voices bursting out into the night, too loud and too giddy and just the exact right amount of alive. The students don't spot Lucas right away, but you can hear it when they do, huge pockets of silence dropping into the noise, as if pieces of the floor have fallen away.

"Get a teacher!" someone shouts.

"Lucas!" a few of them cry. "No! Don't!"

I peer over the edge. There are about a dozen couples there, the girls bright splotches of silk, taffeta, and tulle, the boys shadowlike in their suits. Their faces, all lifted up toward us, are flushed pink from dancing.

"Step down, Brooke!" I say. "Please!"

With one last glance at me, Brooke turns to address the crowd below us.

"I didn't want it to be this way," she calls down to them. "There are some things I have to tell you. And when I do, you'll understand."

The crowd is silent, listening.

"I killed Brooke Lee. I'm the one who bought the drugs for us. I was there, and I lied about it. I pretended to care about her, but I didn't. She was nothing to me. Nothing at—"

"You're wrong," I interrupt. "Lucas cared about you. You're wrong."

Brooke pauses, then shrugs me off, turning back to the crowd below. "That's why tonight I have to—"

"Think about it. How have you been able to inhabit him?" I ask.

"Tonight I have to—" she repeats.

"Because he thought of you, right?"

"To . . . to pay for—"

"How long did it take for him to think of you? Minutes? Seconds? Not even an hour, I bet."

"I have to—"

"Isn't that proof? He thinks about you all the time. He cared."

She stops. The crowd rustles and murmurs. But she turns away from them, the audience below, and faces me. "I'm sorry," she says. "But I have to."

And with that, she steps off the roof.

I'm not quick enough to stop Brooke from jumping off the roof. But I am quick enough to throw myself half over the ledge, my arms instinctively reaching. After months of touching nothing, I expect my hands to remain empty. After all, I'm dead and gone. I can't touch anything, certainly not the arm of a boy falling through the sky.

Somehow, though.

Somehow.

On my death spot, the only place where I can touch the world, and the world me . . . my hand closes on his.

When I grab Lucas's hand, his shoulder makes a popping sound and Brooke howls. But I hold on. The moment holds, too: me stretched over the edge of the roof, Lucas hanging below. The crowd draws a breath that sucks all the noise away, leaving Lucas swaying from side to side in a pocket of silence and space.

Then, the moment breaks. Brooke looks up at me through Lucas's eyes. Her face crumples, and she lifts a hand to mine, grabs on tight.

"Save him," she says.

Together we pull him onto the roof.

25: HOW BROOKE DIED

EVAN ARRIVES ON THE ROOF JUST BEFORE THE OTHERS. HE
finds me kneeling on the ledge, my hand still clasped in Lucas's
hand, Brooke's hand. Lucas has curled himself up into a ball, his
head dropped to his chest, his face pale and waxen as carved soap.

"Please," I say when I see Evan. "I don't want to do this." I nod to
our clasped hands. "I don't want to . . . but I'm scared to let them go."

"It's okay," Evan says. He kneels next to me. "Brooke?" he says
softly. No response.

"She's still in there. She's got to be, but my hand, Evan. I
don't want to hold her hand. She . . . what she did . . . I can't hold
her hand."

"You can let go now," he says.

"Can I? Because—"

"Paige. You're done now. You can let go."

I pull my hand free and climb from the ledge. As I do, I glance
down at my classmates' upturned faces, flushed and animated. Usha
stands at the front of the crowd, her hands knotted at her chest,

her fierce gaze on Lucas's hunched back, as if she could hold him up there with the power of her eyes alone. Jenny stands on one side of her, Chris Rackham and Whitney Puryear on the other, their arms all around one another's backs. At the far edge of the crowd, Kelsey leans against Wes, his arms and coat around her bare shoulders, his chin resting on the top of her head. I feel the memory of those arms around my shoulders, and they warm me, even though they're just a memory, just ghosts. I scan the crowd, and there are dozens and dozens of other faces. They're standing vigil, and I don't think it's because he is Lucas Hayes; I think it's because he is one of them. One of us.

I retreat to the doorway just as Mr. Fisk is coming through it, followed by a couple of Lucas's friends from the basketball team. Mr. Fisk stops, staring at Lucas, hunched over on that ledge. Evan looks up sharply, as if someone has called to him. He walks over to Mr. Fisk until he stands just in front of him and then, with a look of wonder, steps into him, disappearing.

"Evan?" I say.

Mr. Fisk gives a small nod and then, without a word, crosses the roof and encloses Lucas in his arms. When he has him, Mr. Fisk starts crying, his broad shoulders shaking with his sobs. In his arms, Lucas is shaking, too. "You're okay now," he says. "I've got you. You're okay."

Mrs. Morello and Principal Bosworth come up from the stairwell and stand by Lucas's friends. The ambulances set up their call in the distance, but none of us turns to look for their lights. Instead, we stand there and watch them in silence, the man holding the boy. The man is the age Evan would be had he lived; the boy, the age he was when he died.

. . .

"When I woke up, the first thing I found out is that I was dead," Brooke says, all bravado gone from her voice so that it is left small and sad, little more than a whisper.

It's been two weeks since the dance, and I've finally agreed to talk with her, but only if Evan is there, and only if we meet in front of Usha's mural, where I feel safe.

"The second thing I found out is that nothing had happened to the boys who'd killed me. No"—she frowns—"worse. Everyone thought Lucas was a hero. And then, a couple months after, he started up with you." She finally meets my eyes, but I can't look at hers. I turn to the mural, its colors, its shapes. "I didn't hate you," she says. "I didn't ever hate you. I felt sorry for you. Because he was tricking you, like he did me.

"I thought I could warn you. I would try to touch your shoulder sometimes, your hand, to try to get your attention. And I would think, *Stay away from him. He's bad. He's using you.* You never felt me. Never heard me. Until that day on the roof "

"*That's* what you were doing?" I burst out. "Trying to warn me?"

"You don't have to believe me."

But, something about the way she says it, I do believe her.

"Then suddenly that day on the roof, I *was* you. At first, I didn't know what was happening. I thought it was my imagination or a dream or something," she continues. "But then I saw Lucas standing there across the roof, grinning at you. I wanted to scare him. I wanted . . . I was so angry. I was thinking you'd break a leg. I was thinking—"

"I died," I tell her.

"I know."

"Of course you do," I say bitterly. "You know better than anyone."

And now she's the one who can't meet my eyes.

"What happened next?" Evan prompts.

"Nothing," she tells her clasped hands. "I didn't know how to do it again, how to get inside someone. Not until you figured out that it's when they think of us. I understood it then, what had happened with you on the roof, that if I could be you, I could be other people. I could be him."

I look to Evan, startled. *I* had told her. *I'd* given her the key.

She puts her hands over her face, then drops them to her lap forlornly. "I promised myself just Lucas. Nothing big, nothing like the roof. Just little stuff. I got him suspended."

"You messed with that burner girl," I say.

"And Lucas wouldn't have done that?" she asks, adding, "He just wouldn't have asked her to prom."

"But what about Harriet?" Evan says.

"And Heath?" I say.

"I didn't mean it to happen like that," she says.

"Seems like a lot of things didn't happen the way you meant them to," I observe.

"I was scared, so scared of you finding out. And Harriet was saying things that you could have . . . I just wanted her to leave the school. So I would be safe. And Heath, I was just going to—"

"Scare him?" I ask sarcastically.

"He deals to middle-schoolers, did you know that? Eleven, twelve-year-olds?" She pauses, sighs. "But the car was supposed to stop. It should have stopped. Heath would've been scared. Harriet would've been sent back to Greenvale."

"Why didn't it?" Evan asks.

"She saw me. Harriet did. When I got inside her, she knew I was there. She fought me. She kept *pushing* at me. I couldn't get my foot on the pedal."

"But at the prom, with Lucas," I say in as even a voice as I can muster, "you weren't just trying to scare him."

"No," she admits. "I wanted to hurt him. Like I was hurt. It's just that it doesn't stop, the anger, the pain, hating others, hating yourself."

"It stops," I say. "It stops when you decide to stop it."

"I'm glad you saved him." She bows her head. "I am."

I stand and cross to the mural.

"Paige?" Brooke says, meek and wretched, but I'm not listening to her. I'm listening to them.

They're whispering to me again, the warm voices, so warm that they sound like they're singing my name. They sound far away, yet not far at all. I've been hearing them since the night of the dance, every time I visit the mural. What are they saying? I place my hand near the painted wall, then through it. There it is again, the sensation I felt before—sugar dissolved into water, music dissolved into air, the universe dissolved into stars and sky and worlds.

"Paige?" Brooke says, even meeker. "Can you forgive me?"

I take my hand from the wall, hold it tight in my other hand.

"No," I tell Brooke. "I can't forgive you."

Her face falls. "Yeah," she mutters, "I knew that."

"Not yet," I say. "Not right now."

I look to Evan, who nods.

"But," I say, thinking of those voices, the sound of them, "I choose to try."

26: GRADUATION DAY

MRS. MORELLO ARRANGES A SMALL GATHERING FOR THE unveiling of the mural—just Usha, Mr. Fisk, Brooke's parents, and mine. It is, in fact, the perfect number of attendees; everyone who should be there is.

But when Brooke sees her parents, she backs to the far end of the hall and stares at them longingly. She braids her ponytail, unbraids it, braids it, unbraids it, as if it is she and not the hair that is constantly binding and unraveling. I find a little forgiveness in the twists of her hair.

I stand next to my parents, whose hands are knotted in each other's. Usha and Mr. Fisk each take one end of the drop cloth and pull, the sheet billowing out before floating to the ground. The mural is in front of us. My parents cry, but they smile while they cry. My name sings off them, their thoughts blending into one voice. The first voices ever to say my name, I realize, the first ones to think it.

I say their names back to them.

"Mom," I say, "Dad."

"Paige," their thoughts say back to me.

We call each other's names into the silence of the hall, and suddenly the hall isn't silent anymore.

Sometimes, in those last weeks of school, students still come and stand in front of the mural—biblicals, well-rounders, testos, burners, ponies, whoever—and study it. Sometimes one of them thinks my name. Sometimes I don't know what they're thinking, just that it isn't about me. But it doesn't matter if they are thinking of me or not, because Usha was thinking of me when she painted it. Once I stopped getting in the way of her painting it, that is. She'd created something infused with memories of me, of grief and loss. But also of letting go. Of moving on.

It's a warm Saturday in June when Evan, Brooke, and I watch the seniors, shiny columns in their graduation robes, cross the length of the gym and share hearty handshakes with Principal Bosworth. Usha wears a mortarboard decorated with every trinket and medium from Mr. Fisk's room. Wes and Kelsey lean across their folding chairs and make out until Mrs. Morello swats them with a program to get them to stop. Harriet sits in the front row, blinking rapidly, as if she'd woken up from her coma just this morning instead of a month ago. A seizure, they'd finally decreed, had caused her to lose control of the car. Close enough. Heath isn't at graduation. His parents have chosen to homeschool him, especially after the other matter of the drugs Lucas had told Principal Bosworth about. And in fact, Lucas is at graduation, even if he isn't graduating with the rest of our class. He sits up in the stands with his parents, looking more like the Lucas that I'd known, his posture an easy slouch, his blue eyes lazy and laughing. At the end of the ceremony, when the newly named graduates throw their hats in the air, he is the first to stand up and cheer. The hats' golden tassels flip up into the air like miniature suns before reaching an apex and falling back to the ground.

After graduation, Lucas weaves through polite clusters of relatives and rows of vacated folding chairs. He catches the billowing sleeve of Usha's robe, and she turns with a slightly surprised "Hey."

"Hey. Congratulations."

"Thanks." She pulls at the tassel on her hat. "Are you—?"

"Maybe. After summer school."

"Good luck, then." She starts to turn away.

"Wait. That night on the roof. When I . . . when I . . ."

"When you went stargazing?" she finishes with raised eyebrows.

"Yeah," Lucas agrees gratefully. "When I went stargazing. I don't remember much of it. I mean it's all kind of hazy, but . . . but you knew Paige, right? You were her friend, right?"

"Her best friend," Usha corrects him.

"This is going to sound crazy, but up there on the roof, I think— I don't know—but I think, she's the reason I didn't jump. I think maybe she was up there with me. I felt . . ." He turns his hand palm up, looks at it. "I don't know."

Usha combs out the strands of her tassel, watching him carefully.

"Crazy, right?" he says.

Usha shrugs. "Maybe not. Who knows what happens after life? I mean, I'm not ruling anything out."

"Not ruling anything out." Lucas grins. "I like that." He turns to go, but then stops and turns back. "I knew her, you know. Paige."

Usha tilts her head. "You did?"

"Yeah. I liked her. She was rude and sweet and cranky and funny and . . . she was just . . . I don't know . . . she was just the type of girl you'd want to know." He frowns. "I still don't understand what made her—"

"Stop," Usha says. "What you said before? Stop there. That was Paige."

He nods. "Yeah, you're right. That was Paige."

With graduation over, the school is still but for the quiet sweep of the custodian's push broom, the metal slide of a filing cabinet, the infrequent clack of a teacher's heels. The school is ours again, us dead kids. We stand in front of the mural.

Evan tilts his head skeptically. "I don't feel anything."

"Be patient," I tell him. "Be quiet."

I look down at the little dark moth in the corner. Usha painted the wall for Brooke and for me, but I painted that moth for Evan. I hope it's enough.

"Brooke?" I ask, leaning forward to see her on Evan's other side. She shakes her head. "No. Nothing."

"What are we looking for?" Evan asks.

"I don't know." I let my eyes wander from bird's feather to dragonfly eye to plane propeller to dragon's forked tongue. "It's like how the death spots feel firm, this feels the opposite. It feels like . . . it feels like—I don't know—like clouds dissolving into sunlight, like seeds blowing on the wind, like laughter catching between friends, like—"

"Life," Evan suggests. "At least how I remember it."

"Yeah, maybe like that. Maybe like life."

"Wait," Brooke says, her voice a cracked whisper. "Listen."

Evan and I hush. At first, it's a murmur, but as I listen, it grows into a chorus, into a crowd—not one voice but hundreds, thousands, all calling my name. It's like everyone I ever knew is thinking about me, remembering the best thing they could. It's like everyone I ever knew is calling my name, calling me to come meet them.

I turn to Evan. "Do you hear it?"

He says, "They're saying my name."

"What do we do?" I ask.

But it's Brooke who answers, backing up a step, and then with one last look at me, running forward and throwing herself through the wall. Except she doesn't go through it, and she doesn't hit it. For a moment, it's as if she's become a part of the mural, a vivid collection of colors and shapes, but also a girl. Then she's gone.

"A life spot," Evan breathes.

"Are you scared?" I say. "I'm scared."

Evan nods. "But I'm ready. Are you?"

I take a last look at the empty hallway. I turn to Evan. "Together?"

We step forward.